Apprentice

Book 1 of Sen of the Woods

‹‹‹•›››

Mab Morris

The full trilogy of Sen of the Woods
is dedicated to Alex Levy.
For all the years we explored the woods together!

Contents

‹‹‹◆›››

Book of Spring

Chapter One

The month of Thielle, early spring

S pring waters bit my hands as payment for the divine white clay I was digging. My lower back ached as I lifted another handful into the tightly woven basket beside me. Apprentice work. Master Tages and his adept, Cai, used this clay during healing Medicine.

I had been with Tages since last autumn, the day after Grandmother Turani had disappeared for the last time, this time not wandering, but guided.

Tages had come to fetch me by her design, so that I could further my education beyond her ancient Ndeb herb lore. With her dementia, had she known that she'd sent me to study what I now knew was a dying craft?

Spring is a time of growth, a promise of abundance—yet all I could think of this morning was death, dying, or damage. Dead leaves blanketed the cold winter earth, their decay fueling future growth.

During one of my foraging walks in the month of Leinth,

the death of autumn, I came across a broken branch. Its pale wood was wet, and water slowly *drip, drip*, dripped from the wound. The tree's last drink in late autumn was betrayed by an unexpected breath of winter. The early freeze cracked the tree's weakness during the night with ice. Morning's warmth let it weep onto my hands.

Icy water pooled into my palms like tears. A tree, like the World Tree, with a living side and destruction on the other, or one dead branch. It was hard not to see it as symbolic: I was a person, caught between life and death of the world around me, with forces that betray us into weeping where we break. My heart was broken.

I did not know what had happened to the woman who had raised me, not really.

The vocation chosen for me, similar to what I'd already learned from Grandmother Turani... this vocation was dying. Few people practiced it, or practiced it with integrity. She had at least sent me to study with one of the greatest Doctor-Diviners in the land. I enjoyed Tages's curious mind. I shared in his curiosity and embraced books and knowledge beyond our craft's traditional scope. But what would I have when my studies ended, and I was a Master Doctor-Diviner?

I put another scoop of sacred clay into the basket and wondered how chemistry would reduce this clay. Maybe it would pick out its antiseptic components, or some other sort of useful compound? I doubted it could detect the touch of divine grace. Science lacked Medicine. While it might pick out an herb's effective components, it was well... merely Medicine.

I tried not to groan as I bent back down with that thought and with my stiffening back. It would have been far easier to kneel in the creek, wet to the chest, but it was too cold this early in spring. This cold would seize my chest like a vise. If given a chance, I'd probably float in the waters to cool the inflammation. Cai might not want to wait while I did. He was somewhere in the woods where I heard one lone jackal cackling. It wasn't looking at Cai and his somewhat illegal rabbit traps. I felt its eyes upon me.

Jackal and Crow had paced my path even as a child. They were nearer, or louder of late. Pointed. Mocking. Laughing. Waiting for me to do something.

I bent back down and put both hands into the water.

Jackal's laughing didn't distract me from my thoughts. At least not for long. Aule had left to study at a university up north, instead of studying with his father. He had written that the school of anatomy was once a temple to the Goddess Nhor. He said what had become of Thielle's temple was worse. It was now a temple of prostitution. Thielle for the beauty of life? No longer. Her ugly twin, Nhor, remained a goddess for the dead. Many gods were now largely remembered merely by the names of months.

With my fingers pruned from winter's melting ice, I pondered this change of an Age. There were times it felt as if we were in the winter of dying gods—hopefully readying for a spring of new, as yet unknown ones. Who might they be?

I was caught within this change. Maybe the change from one generation of Divinity to the next, but definitely between Medicine and science. What was I to do with it? I was at least forewarned. I didn't need divination to see it.

A spring caw like a laugh from a crow startled me from my musings, and I let the clay draw my attention again. The clay was hard-packed to my cold, stiffened fingers. They ached curling into the deposit, but as I drew it up, it became soft, silky in my fingers. Clouds of white flowed down the creek, like memories of ice.

I eased my back and put another handful of silky white into a tightly woven basket.

Grandmother Turani had asked me to learn all I could of all Three Rivers of Knowledge, to bind them before a tree died. Which tree, I did not know. She had been getting confused by then. Tages explained this disordered mind was a mark of old age.

I gathered more clay. If the waters were near freezing, it was still better to gather the clay before the rising hysteria of Goddess Thielle's weeping overwhelmed the banks of the creek— and certainly before the Apatin followed Her weeping rain with His torrential storms.

Using the clay, I drew the symbol of an adept Doctor-Diviner on my left hand, and then the master on the right. I let both water and clay wash them away. Water: it cleans. It destroys. It heals.

The month of Thielle is for the Goddess of Beauty in the season of spring, when snowmelt swells the waters before the coming of spring rain. Her weeping helps flowers burst forth from their winter's sleep to crown Thielle with a riot of flowers and colors and scents after her grief. I looked up at the bank to ease my back from all the bending and twisting.

As if I were waking from my grumpiness, I noticed beauty. Nearby, early bell-like blossoms, white with the memory of the dusting of snow that had birthed them. They bowed over the whitened waters, under the light green canopy above, insipid still, hiding their future fullness.

I bowed, stirred the silting clay, and let go of my frustrations. "Weep clean, O Spring, the darkness of Winter past, and let grief turn to joy!" I said.

I bent back to my work, filling a second tightly woven

basket with the special clay. Wind played on the branches above, giving a soft murmuration. I hummed with it and began to sing words.

"One was wrapped
In lace and gold
Another leaves and dirt
One died in the cold
The other death did skirt

Oh, the humble child..."

I mumbled this last line again, looking for the next part, but it did not come. There was more I couldn't remember, except that the humble child was special somehow.

"Sen, do you have enough yet?" Cai called from the embankment.

I started, nearly tipping the basket into the stream. "Yes," I said. "I put one basket by that tree. I hope you can carry it."

He snorted. "Of course. What were you singing?"

"Oh, a lullaby, I think. Grandmother Turani used to sing it to me. I can't remember all the words."

"It doesn't sound familiar. Isn't it a bit dark for a lullaby, with one twin dead?"

"Well, that's, umm, yes. Pretty dark." My heart pounded a moment as I wondered what that song might mean. Why had she sung it to me? There were other, more restful lullabies in the world. I shook my head and looked up at Cai again.

Tages's adept was well boned and tall, with the white adept mark on one hand. Despite his white cape-like tebenna wrapped around his torso and the wide pantaloons, both stained at the hems, he looked strong enough to be a hunter, especially with the brace of rabbits he carried. He noticed me looking at the white adept scar on his hand.

"Don't worry. You'll get your scars," he said. He ran his hand through his wavy brown hair, shaking off the spatter of water that had graced him from the tree canopy above. It had rained overnight, and what had greened was still delicate, pale, but dripped at the slightest breeze.

Cai shook his head. "I know you miss Turani. Things must change for people to grow and learn," he said. "You need... life experience. Here, you will gain that, and more."

"More?"

He laughed, noting my tone. "You know a good deal, I won't deny, of herbs, of lore, but you're still..."

"Yes. More. It's people I must learn."

We both heard a noise up the hill, and Cai dropped his rabbits and kicked some leaves over them, even before he turned to look. He moved to pick up the basket near him and then put it down almost on top of them.

"Kutu!" I said, in both greeting and informing Cai that his instinct in hiding his rabbits was correct. He turned and waved at the hunter.

"I see you have been hunting, young Cai," Kutu said, coming down the hill, moving like a panther. He wore leather. "Why do you let Sen gather up the clay by herself?"

Cai shrugged. It wasn't his job to do the grunt work.

"Good snares you put out," Kutu said. Cai tried not to preen with pride. "Do you have any salves for some scratches?"

Cai and I looked at his leg as he made his way down the hill, and noted that his 'scratches' were more like gashes. Proud hunter that he was, the wounds did not slow him down.

"Help me out of the stream, Cai. This is the last of the clay I can get with these baskets, anyway," I said. "I have supplies in my bag."

"If you put his rabbits in your bag when you are done, I'll say nothing about it," Kutu said with a grin.

I grinned back. I'd met few people at Grandmother Turani's, but Kutu was one of them, moving his herds in a wider, more dangerous circuit during warmer weather. His meat profited in flavor with the wider range of herbs. Being a bit of a distance from Tages's compound, he'd come by a time or two, relying on Turani for herbs and healing. Kutu and I had often exchanged information, skittering over the boundaries of Thefarland tradition a time or two. There had to be some fluidity in such traditional roles, for hunters could not always find a ready Doctor-Diviner in the wild. If they once had, no longer. There were herbs and other things we needed that hunters could find in their work.

While I cleaned up the gash on Kutu's leg, Cai stowed his rabbits in my bag.

"Had the injury happened farther away..." I started to say.

"I mean, you do watch cattle farther afield, don't you?" Cai asked.

"You do remember how to clean it?" I asked.

"Yes, but I noticed you earlier," Kutu said. "So I came here instead. I slipped on some rocks while killing a snake." He held up a snake. Deadly. Kutu was one of the better hunters. "I did not have the herbs for the poultice, or a ready wrap. Also, Jackal was nearby, and while I discouraged him from coming this way, I thought I'd warn you in case a pack followed."

"I heard him," I said, remembering his laughter earlier.

Kutu's eyebrows raised.

Cai said, "I didn't hear them."

Jackals and lions roamed the area. A bane in cattle land, but apparently a strange boon in the grain lands. From what I'd heard, the lions knew deer enjoyed those crops. Farmers knew that while deer could decimate a field in a night, they were lions' dinner at dusk. Easy prey for the lazy creatures.

This was dairy land. Thefarland was one of the primary sources of the cheese predominant in the cooking of the entire region, pairing beautifully with the breads, pastas, beans, and wines most of the southern region had become famous for in the past generation. Here, the lions worked harder to get to the cattle hunters protected. The hunter's role was dangerous often enough that they needed our services. Their trade was our primary source of meat. Kutu was getting healing, trading only a blind eye to Cai's kills.

I finished up my ministrations, and Kutu said he would bring Tages more mushrooms. We thanked him and then picked up our baskets of clay and went on our way.

As he was leaving, I asked Cai, "Don't Tages and Velia have plenty of mushrooms left?" I knew there was quite a store of dried ones for stew.

"Not that's grown on cattle dung. Tages will be needing some soon to test you, if you replace me in the divination part of an adept's work."

"What does that mean?"

"You'll see." After a bit, Cai said glumly, "He'll have us dissecting them, you know."

I knew he was talking about rabbits, not mushrooms. Cai liked to eat his food, not study it. Tages always had us studying the innards of animals, even if we were to eat them.

"I don't know why he does this. It's new since you've been here. I could have gone to Jambrone if I'd wanted to study anatomy."

"You could have waited for hunters to trade with us instead of snaring rabbits."

"And then we'd be eating snake tonight," he said. "They at least gut their meat before they give it to us more often than not."

I stumbled, catching an insight almost like walking into a web in the woods. "Something tells me we'll be doing something else instead of cutting up rabbits before we make a stew."

"Are you sure you've not gone through the adept test yet?" He sniggered.

I glared at him.

"Well, I hope you're right, even if no ancestors guided you," Cai said with some cheer. "Why can't we just skin it and roast it, instead of identifying its inner parts?"

"You're only complaining because you still can't identify the liver or the lungs," I said.

"No. I'm only complaining because I'm hungry! And you're one to talk!" said Cai. "You're avoiding making cheese."

"She sent me."

Like Aule, I didn't sense any of my ancestors. This made any household work with her a bit like hidden thorns in a bundle of roses. Dead roses, mind you, to gather the hips for Medicine. Velia wouldn't waste anything that useful. I hadn't hesitated when she'd sent me.

"Oh," Cai said. "Well, I was glad to get out as well. We've been studying hard this past winter. It's far more book reading than my old mentor ever gave me."

"Well, we were sent out to get this clay, so even had I

wanted to stay and work with Velia, I did have to go," I said. "She told me that Tages divined it will be a wet enough spring."

"He's rarely wrong, but why did you have to pick the farthest deposit?"

"Lazy bones. You could have helped me gather clay instead of getting rabbits. Now you'll have a long walk and a rabbit anatomy lesson—well, at least at some point."

He groaned.

I laughed. As we made our way back to the main road, I thought of Cai's work with Tages. I understood that even prior to Mastery, Cai had been doing more of the mystical work. The healing we did often had more of his divining hand, with Tages trusting Cai's dreams and divination rather than his own.

Having met other Doctor-Diviners, I was glad that Tages would train me. Cai was more than competent. I looked forward to Tages trusting me as much with divination.

When Aule sent books, Tages and I pored over these books and examined the drawings within. The book on anatomy by a scholar named Vesalus had anatomical drawings of human bodies that helped us understand the body, which dissected rabbits and other animals could not clarify. We rarely had opportunities to do any kind of surgery to look inside. After a person was dead, we were bound to leave their body in peace, or risk all our Medicine if the spirit of the deceased became angry for the disrespect.

Vesalus's book proved Tages's belief that the ancient writings of a man named Galen were erroneous. Tages chortled quite a bit while reading it, delighted that his own dislike of Galen was justified. Vesalus's book delighted our mentor to no end. He began a correspondence with the man on the strength of it. These letters helped further illuminate our knowledge of what Tages knew and understood, comparing it to the dissection of animals that had steered so many healers—including many Doctor-Diviners —wrong.

Cai had some training with another Doctor-Diviner before studying with Tages. When that man died, his choices of excellent teachers were Zelia to the north and Tages. She had been too far from his home village, so he had come here.

Soon after we reached the main road, we met a servant on the path. She stopped and said, "Lord Thefare's niece, Hastia, is ill. Your master said you would all come." She hurried on before we could do more than offer casual greetings back.

When we entered the round house, Velia was stirring a soup of meat and beans. The aroma of cooking herbs filled the room. She turned to us as we entered the door. Her high-boned cheeks were red from the heat of the fire, her thick, dark brown hair curling with the damp of her sweat. She looked like a voluptuous figurine of Thielle.

"You're back! Good. We've a lot to do. Sen, help me hang the saddlebow cheese, please. You are grown taller than me."

Cai took his rabbits to Tages, who hung them outside, and then led him into the workroom where they would consult. I could hear Tages give him a list of minor doctors to go collect, loading him up with his drum and vestments as he talked. He'd have chores for me, as well. I stood on a stool and hung cheese. I made sure to hang them evenly over the rafter, like bags off a saddlebow.

"Velia, if it is Hastia who is ill, ought it not be part of your work? Women's healing?" I asked.

"Perhaps, but you are a young woman. I want to..." Her pause was slight as she grimaced. "Tages wants to see how you work together. You'll do the diagnosis—without divination, of course."

As I was not an adept, I could not do divination. "Of course," I said.

"And you will do the soft cast on her body and her night shift or slip and the walls."

I nodded.

"Feel the cheese, make sure they have the proper shape," she said.

There were two pairs of cheeses Velia would sell and a smaller one for the household. Even as I hung the second pair, I could see the first slowly begin to form its distinctive pear shape on either side of the beam. She had several of the smaller Dolica cows, tended by one of her cousins in the Hunter Cult. She let them roam as wild as she could for better flavor, trusting her cousin Thocero to guard them. The cheese was renowned because of it.

A few days before, I'd dried and cleaned the fourth stomach of one of her calves she'd sold to the castle. I'd done the butchering as well, with Cai's help, while Tages had given us an anatomy lesson in the process. While the men carried the meat to the castle, I'd put the stomach in with some whey and some of the distinctive wine Velia made. I'd filtered the resulting rennet this morning before leaving to get clay.

When she used veal rennet, the cheese was delicate, especially as the milk of her cows was fragrant with gentian, strawberry, and licorice. The goat rennet made a sharper cheese. The milk was from Tages's goats. Their milk and cheeses were rich in the scent of rosemary and sage, but sometimes hints of acacia if he'd set up his goats to get the encroaching shrubs before they grew their sharp thorns. I lifted one of them down for her.

"I'll sell it tomorrow. Tingasa asked for some," Velia was saying, reaching up to take it from my hands.

Tages came into the room, pulling on his beard in thought. They sometimes seemed like such a mismatched pair, just on sight. He was slender, stoop-shouldered from reading and working in his laboratory. His wispy black hair had started to go gray just at the temples and along his high forehead.

Velia was well-rounded in ways that made her more than feminine. She could have been a study of mother goddesses, with healthy breasts and wide hips, though she'd only had one child. Apparently by choice, and as proof of her ability with womanly arts.

"Lord Thefare's niece is ill," Tages said, looking up at me.

"Yes," I said.

"You will go and prepare her."

"What herbs shall I take?" I asked, reaching for another pair of cheeses from Velia to hang.

"I think I know what's needed," he said. "Ask Velia."

I knew Velia had a good idea what was going on with the girl. She was well acquainted with Hastia's mother, Arntlei, who was part of Velia's family through their great-great-grandmother, Lady Vastia. I knew Tages would gain more knowledge, if needed, through his divination.

With a start, I realized that neither he nor Cai had done any divination to confirm any probable diagnosis. I hadn't heard the threshing basket he used for divination the whole time I helped with the cheeses. Using his threshing sticks, engraved with various symbols, out in the courtyard, had a distinct sound. I wondered if I should take note of this. It felt odd.

Velia prattled on about bladder infections and menstrual

cramps, while she assembled herbs and tonics that would be useful for either ailment.

Velia set me to put the gathered clay into a larger fired clay pot. Then she ordered me to gather up more cooking herbs and cut some onions to put into the soup pot. The long walk had left me hungry, and the scent of her cooking always made my mouth water.

Tages came back inside and began to look through the dried herbs and vials of extracts, loading them into my bag. Each vial was carefully padded to prevent breakage, especially as there was a small ceramic jar with blessed white clay, and the brushes I would use to paint both Hastia and her mother, as well as the walls of the room.

Tages and Velia consulted quietly, and then he ordered me to move along, apparently content with her choices.

Chapter Two

<><>

The road to the town and castle was not a long one. My wild-crafting journeys were often longer. It was cool enough not to leave me in a sweat, but Cai and I had walked far that morning.

I freshened up in a stream close to home to give myself and my dampened clothes time to dry. A crow called out with that eerie sound that heralded spring. Something not a caw. I shivered at the sound and looked up. I knew that branch, that tree. A bird of death on a dead branch. It was *more* than just a bird. Crow had an amber gem in its beak that it tossed and caught. It moved up and down the broken branch, laughing at me.

This crow seemed to speak more than words, but like the wind whistling through the wattles during my childhood, I did not know the tongue. It laughed again, perching near the break of the branch for a moment, then went back to focus on its bauble.

I turned from the stream, and Crow murmured and played with its gem behind me. I went back to the road that led to the

Women's Compound, shivering not only from the dampness of my clothes.

I took a shortcut off the path and climbed one of the large granite outcrops. From here, I could see the landscape. I looked to the northwest, where I'd grown up. I grew up between both landscapes. Between trees and scrubland. Somewhere there was a tree where Grandmother Turani had found me. One day, I would find it. Maybe find my mother and father, and find out why they'd wanted me to die of exposure. I could see the rivers of budding green flowing toward the north and east, where there was more water, onwards to the sea.

To the west and south, the landscape was far more scrub before one reached savanna. I looked toward Thefare's castle. From this vantage, I could see a carpet of fading white blossoms giving way to budding leaves, still pale against fragile green canopies with dots of darker green. The white was acacia, and there were winters where this was our only hint of anything like snow, with the petals on the ground. This thorny wattle was valued in cattle country. We used it for needles. Hunters used the branches to build quick fences when herds of cattle or sheep were moved from one graze or village. Lions would have to be famished to risk impaling their furry skin.

Growing up, I used to think the whistling wattle was nature singing to the Divine in their own tongue. On windy nights, they were my other lullaby. Nature and the Divine intermingled, like Crow and Nhor, Thielle and her winged attendant, Achivizer. I yearned to understand the songs they sang. Now I know that ants made their homes in some of the long spines, turning their base bulbous. At the holes where the ants made entrance, the wind turned the wattles into flutes.

Apprentice

Like the granite outcrops dotted throughout that landscape, wild olives mingled with acacia and other trees and brush, a burst of darker green. Their fruit, small and dry, their flavors, harsh. They were drought-resistant, and cultivars were often grafted to their roots. These were a promise of a future, if one planted olives and nurtured them. One would never see the fruit in one's own lifetime. Olive trees were planted for a grandchild's future.

The trees made way to grasslands with one substantial granite outcropping, where Thefare's castle perched, like a break against the trees, and the landscape flowed into scrubbier land and grass. From this rock, I could see the forest greens fade to scrub and savanna, and how the season's change had altered the land.

I climbed down my outcrop of dark stone and made my way toward the square building on a large, rounded outcrop of granite.

Thefare's castle was not hard to see from the approach to the town. It had recently been renovated with a modern style found in the cities. This castle was pillared and rectangular. The angles, sharp. I hoped the building was considered beautiful elsewhere. It did not quite suit the granite below it, nor most of the sprawling town around it.

Grandmother Turani's home, and many of the older buildings in the region, had been built within boulders like these, with some of the pale stones also common to the region to add to their structure as walls. These and the common roundhouses echoed the rolling nature of the countryside.

Velia said that the compound supported the castle.

She told stories about how Thefare's great-great-grandmother's wealth had been the reason the land had once been rich.

Some said the compound was below the acropolis, so Thefare could look down at the women. It was a nasty thought, and yet I could see that reflected in daily life. There had been a time when wealth went from mother to daughter—they had the homes, whereas men had hunting. The Hunting Cult had largely become defenders of cattle, but some hunters now even owned houses.

That change had come as the area grew in wealth with cattle, especially after Thefarland had the only healthy cattle in the region. It wasn't the boon that Thefare, and the men of his land— even Tages, who had saved them—first thought. In the lands of neighboring lords, hunters and desperate need turned pasture lands into fields of grain. They began a trend. Now, many local men owned their own crumbling homes and grumbled at the thought of how rich the surrounding grain lands had become.

Inside the walled compound, the round houses and carved bricks of the enclosure echoed the pale earth of the landscape. It was wedded to the huge dark stone boulders that guarded the entrance. The sturdy buildings had a beauty that married structure and nature together. Inside the walls, buildings were often painted with vibrant colors. Traditional houses were resplendent with symbolic geometric patterns in white, red, and black—colors and shapes echoing the embedded healing lore of Ndeb—but also greens and blues. Many were simple and very stylized, others more intricate, verging on murals. Less traditional frescoes echoed scenes of daily life, myths, and nature. They reflected some connections to the port city to the east or the cities around the great Obronian Lake to the north.

Apprentice

As I walked through the compound, I greeted some of the women who were husbandless despite their wealth. When Velia visited Aule in the great city, she brought back fabrics and tinted drawings of, presumably, the latest fashions. The styles adopted here were most likely outdated. Thankfully, regional and traditional dress remained.

One woman walked past with a bodice lifting up her breasts, but it was one she'd embroidered to match the hem of the veil that hung on either side of her head and a skirt that moved freely. It was a glory of basic, unbleached cloth embroidered in patterns of flowers in reds and oranges, echoing older patterns.

I nodded at her, knowing that she was a woman, at least, with a rich imagination, embracing both old and new, and doing it skillfully. Her return nod was given with a fixed smile. My plain apprentice robes, I was sure, with all their use in woodlands, garden, and sick rooms, were worn. I looked a trifle shabby.

Throughout the compound, I could easily see the slow cultural shifts that had started with the wealth of cattle and then their decline. I saw it in the art as well as the clothing. Some of the bodices looked clearly made over from older, less fashionable clothes.

I passed Velia's large one-story house and the added private garden enclosure. On the outer walls, amid the elaborate frescoes she'd had redone after a trip to visit Aule, I could pick out the remaining traditional diamond pattern of a married woman, the horizontal growing symbol of a skillful person, and symbols noting the number of her cows—yet more triangles displaying her wealth against the base patterns of her pride. Velia let her cousin Thocero use the house she'd inherited through her mother's line because she now lived with Tages. Thocero guarded Velia's cows and brought us meat.

I made my way to the ostentatious two-story structure that had stood the test of time far better than the one that had to be rebuilt on Thefare's acropolis. I liked Arntlei's round building far better than the massive three-story rectangular structure that had been built before the wane of our lord's wealth.

Lady Arntlei and her daughter, Hastia, had lived in the Women's Compound ever since Thefare had banished his brother, Fuluns, years ago in a fit of anger that had apparently not waned. From what I understood, Arntlei had not divorced him but had not felt compelled to join him, either. It was clear to me, however, that she'd lost nothing in her choice. Her home had many rooms, and her and her daughter's rooms were on a second level—daring construction considering the age of the structure.

I was sent up by a servant cooking soup for the second meal of the day. I could tell that it was not nearly as fragrant, nor would it be as flavorful as anything Velia made. There was a servant waiting by the door of Hastia's room, presumably to cater to any needs Hastia would have. She was a little girl named Casiea. I'd met her during an outbreak of a waterborne illness. Hastia had taken her in as a servant when her parents had died from the poisoned wells.

Her face lit up. "Sen! It is you," she said. "You are come!" she whispered. "Her ancestors are so irate."

I smiled gently at her, touching her shoulder in reassurance. I was glad to see that Casiea looked healthy. Meeting her had been during one of the first healing events I'd been part of, mainly staying with her family and giving them water and cleaning up their mess as they slowly died. It had been a dramatic introduction to my studies with Tages and all I'd learned in the past.

There was worry on the girl's face, so I knew that whatever Hastia was going through was unusual. I suddenly became nervous.

"Tages and Velia will be here soon, and the adept is gathering minor doctors," I said.

Casiea nodded.

"I need to prepare Hastia and bathe her. Will you send up clean water? I will also need a fresh shift and bedclothes for your mistress, as well."

Casiea nodded and scuttled off.

I went into the room and saw that Hastia was alone. She soon would not be. For a Doctor-Diviner to do his work on Hastia, who had neither been wed nor had her Milk Tree ritual, her mother, Arntlei, had to be there. Surrounded by family and minor doctors who would dance for Hastia's healing Medicine, both of them would be healed by old Medicine—and new. Tages and his students said little of the latter. Science was not trusted by many in the villages, having the same incomprehensible success as magic to their minds.

I bent down and gently touched the suffering girl. She lay in her bed, curled up over cramps so painful I could see the sweat on her brow. I was glad my hands weren't shaking. I knew my work here was something of a test. An adept was responsible for their own diagnoses and healing, but still under the auspices of their mentor. It seemed unfair to try me out on a girl quite clearly in pain.

My heart pounded, but I told myself to be brave.

I quietly told Hastia that I was there to prepare her. I'd already been informed that the Medicine would be performed in the girl's room and initially had my doubts about that. It was a larger room than I'd expected. It might be a bit cramped with twelve people, but certainly large enough for the ceremony. I was a little bit in awe of this show of wealth.

I began to get my things ready, laying out the pot of clay and herbs that would help freshen the poor girl. The water came up, carried by a different servant, with Casiea bringing the clean shift. I dampened it and blessed it with clay.

"Take this to dry by a fire and bring it back as soon as you can. Knock on the door, please," I told her.

As soon as the door shut, I got to work. I started with Hastia's face, and then took off the old shift, setting it outside the door to be cleaned. It smelled of sweat and an acrid tang of urine that told me much. I quietly thanked both Tages's and Velia's teaching. I used bathing her to examine her body, pressing on her skin lightly to see if there was a cause not identified by Arntlei, who had persuaded Thefare to call upon us.

I gauged the level of her fever and located places of pain. From this initial observation, and that of the household, I could see that the illness was not contagious. I went ahead with the rest of my work. Had it been contagious, I would have painted the doorway for Tages to see.

Tages often had me paint walls with this clay during a Medicine to speak to the ancestors who had afflicted a villager or townsperson, the seen part of our often unseen work as Doctor-Diviners. Ancestors could get angry at being forgotten and plague their families. Symbols painted on walls with the white clay caught their attention.

Studying with Tages, we also tended to illnesses that had little to do with ancestors. There were new ways to see the herb craft Grandmother Turani taught me, or that Tages relied upon. I could not have my hands in the clay and not remember how many times we'd placated ancestral spirits who actually *had* plagued their surviving children. I feared the day when healing focused only on the body, or worse: only a few supposedly *relevant* symptoms, and not the whole nature of a person. But in all honesty, it was all I had.

With white clay, thinned to a slip, I painted symbols on her skin, above her ovaries and bladder, which Tages's science, and Vesalus's book on anatomy had taught me to be able to find with accuracy. These symbols were similar to the geometric shapes painted on houses as a petal to a rose.

With the slight fever and answers to questions about her habits, I guessed that there was more to her pain than her upcoming—supposedly stalled—menses. I happened to know her cycles were not quite regular, despite her age, nor were her breasts developed enough for a ceremony of the Mother Tree, if indeed they chose to celebrate such an ancient rite that would cut her from her mother and make her a woman in her own right and free to marry. Some girls blossomed later than others.

As I painted her, she asked, "Can you paint magic on me so that my breasts grow faster?"

"I can try, but nature must be free." Her shoulders were narrow, her arms and legs bony, coltish. She would possibly grow into those arms and legs—and if so, become stunning.

"Some ancestor must be mad at me for keeping me like a child, even while my body"— she gasped in a cramp—"tries to show I'm a woman."

"You will no doubt marry. My master and the other minor doctors will help you be free of pain," I said.

I felt bad for her. I knew that she was a little older than me. I was certainly well developed enough to marry and bear children, though I had no thoughts of that. I might be bound to Tages till he released me from my apprenticeship, and yet I had far more freedom than she. I was often hunting for and studying herbs and wildlife on my own. Old enough to marry, but not looking it, her family would no doubt adopt the practice of waiting only till she had a good marriage proposal. There were men who liked younger women, and lately, many young women married without any kind of Mother Tree ritual. That ritual waited not only for a girl with regular menses to be able to carry a child, but to nurse a child without taxing the mother too hard.

There were still women and men who protested this kind of abuse of women's health—for girls too young to bear children often died. It was a terrible sign of the times that there were women who valued men's opinions over their health or their daughters' health. Velia's whole household were as equally vociferous as she against girls being married off too young.

There was a knock at the door, so I opened it and accepted the slightly warm, fresh shift. The clay had dried into the cloth just enough to bless it, but not flake.

"Thank you," I said. "We will be ready in a moment." I closed the door.

Carefully so as not to smudge the symbols I'd painted on her, I helped Hastia into the fresh gown. I freshened her wavy black hair and her face, painting symbols on her hands and neck with the clay.

"Thank you. That already feels better," she said.

I smiled. Cleanliness always helps improve the mood of the sick. Having learned a means of moving the patient and still being able to change the sheets, I carefully removed her old bedding and put fresh under her as well. I took the filthy bedclothes to Casiea, still waiting at the door, letting her know that Hastia was presentable. I took the bowl of clay and began to work on the walls.

I painted symbols on the wall that spoke to the ancestors, with a few supposed errors that Tages had taught me to inform him of what only my examination of the girl could tell him. The anatomical images of books gave me a better picture of what was causing her complaint.

If he were not present and without an examination he could not perform except in divination, Tages needed to know what either Cai or I could more easily discover during our evaluation of a patient. In some cases, we could confer quietly; in others, this code worked well. It added to the Medicine's magic and Tages's mystique. It was my first solo examination, and done without either man looking to the ancestors first, as far as I could tell. I was nervous, but Velia had assured me that this would work well enough for Hastia's probable complaints.

I cleaned off the table in her room that Hastia, no doubt, used to prepare herself for the day. Oils and unguents and, for a girl this young, the surprising powders and paints for the face. Matrons used this, or women after their Mother Tree ritual. Velia had some for festival use, but I'd never tried them, and she'd never shared.

I blessed the table and laid out bowls of healing herbs and of colored paint—white, red, and black. Arntlei came into the room. She wore a modern bodice, tight to her body, lifting her breasts, but her skirts were still loose, and she covered herself with thin veils. If she wore paint, it was not dramatic enough to show through the fine cloth. She was followed by Thefare.

I tried not to look surprised. It was not his presence that struck me in a Medicine for a young girl. It was his dress.

Having already seen some signs of change in our land, I ought not to have been surprised. I was. He'd kept the traditional cloth of the region but eschewed the long robes. He'd had them styled fashionably for the cities. The simple cloth—a pale yellow ochre—had traditional embroidery. Those elaborate geometric designs were usually a heavy, but flowing hem or a pattern down the breast for the robes worn by men. Now that border was at the ankle, waist, and collar. It seemed misplaced, and certainly didn't suit his stocky, long-armed frame. The city fashion looked strange in the traditional cloth of the region.

The garish clash of styles might be there merely to prove his superior wealth because people would have to take notice. I schooled my face and turned back to my work.

At first, they were silent. Arntlei went to her daughter and sat behind her on the bed, stroking her, looking at the symbols painted on her daughter that had not been covered up.

"You look familiar," said Thefare, after a while.

I turned to him, in some astonishment. I had believed that while he knew of me, he had never really met me; I was too beneath his notice.

"Who are your parents?" he asked. His strong square jaw, which Hastia had sadly inherited from his family, jutted out at me as he looked down on me, examining me.

I was disconcerted by the intensity of his gaze, but I replied mildly, "I do not know. I was found in the woods by Grandmother Turani."

He laughed. "Old Mother Love," he said. "So, you are the

one who works for Tages called Sen of the Woods?"

"I am."

"I might be able to guess who your parents are. I will have to ask Tages if he knows."

I did not reply. I only bid him step aside so I could sweep the room. To perform the Medicine, the place needed to be clean and ready for Tages and the other minor doctors to dance with our healing chants. While I worked, I also stifled my irritation at his teasing about Turani's name. She *had* loved me, while my parents had left me out to die of exposure. It was not a new jibe; people had often mocked the contrast of an aged woman, older than any other person in the area, and how she was named with one of Thielle's other names: Turan or, in her case, Turani.

Without a Doctor-Diviner's mark, her use of herbs to help and heal was sometimes considered witchcraft. Tages had learned more Ndeb from her, bolstering a fading part of our craft. Her use of herbs had never been random. There was history and knowledge of herbalism embedded in the language used by Doctor-Diviners in their Medicine. At least, for those who bothered to *learn* the language. Turani had been fluent, as was I.

Thefare's wife, Ati, came into the room and stood by him. She did not hide her more city fashion. Her headdress still had a veil, but it fell to either side of her, emphasizing the narrowed waist and lift of her breasts with her embroidered bodice.

The lavenders, pale blues, and pinks declared it was imported. The fraying of some of the softer petals in the embroidery showed that it had been laundered many times.

"You wore it!" said Arntlei, gesturing toward a necklace highlighted by Ati's cleavage.

"It's pretty, isn't it? A nod to the ancestor who left

Thefare's family the original damaged relic. This one's *whole*, and gold!" I noticed the amber pendant dangling in her cleavage. It seemed discordant with the gold.

"Thank you," Arntlei replied. "They say it was made for healing."

Ati shrugged. "The real one is broken, tarnished, and ugly. Hopefully, they like the replacement better. It's a sign of healing they claim the original has. I've never noticed anything."

Arntlei frowned for a moment and then turned to the door, waiting for the primary to arrive.

Tages finally came in, followed by Velia, Cai, and the minor doctors. He began to examine the symbols on the wall as I turned to put on my mask and don the outer layers of my dancing garment. Cai, in his mask and robes, had the great drum. Two other minor doctors, men, had other, smaller drums. They would provide two of the base beats that Cai would elaborate upon. Three women minor doctors—who had presumably suffered the same ailment as Hastia—would dance for this healing rite. Velia did not hand me any rattles or gourds to make music with; I had bells on my wrists and ankles, smaller than those of other minor doctors who shook larger metal bells in their hands.

Velia painted Arntlei to match her daughter, but only on the arms and feet. She blessed the other family members present as well—for it could easily be their neglect of an ancestor that had caused the girl's illness. *It might be her father's*, I thought, sardonically, but there was little we could do about that. We could help Hastia.

Cai began to beat the drum, Tages started the chant, and we began to dance.

The chant was familiar to me and gave me time to look

about and notice the energies. They were already divided, and no wonder the ancestors were peevish. Hardly anyone could focus on the afflicted girl, the dance, or the Medicine. The only thing they all did was sing the chant.

I noted that the sourness of Velia's face was not aimed at me, for once. She was subdued, and as I looked around the room, I noticed Arntlei and Ati could not help but size up Velia's plain—but less laundry-worn—clothing, and its pure tradition. It was completely appropriate for her role here. Velia didn't wear fashion outside the healing dances. Tages had too strong an opinion on what those laced bodices did to a woman's body. Velia could only tersely remind him that childbearing did far more moving and compressing of a woman's innards than any outer garment could ever do.

As the women danced, none of the women noted how Thefare gazed at the lifted breasts of the corseted women, nor how Ati ignored her husband's frank gaze at her bosom. She only touched her necklace or gazed at the jewels on her arms or fingers. I sighed. One of the women dancers wore a bodice, and her liberal glances at Thefare and Cai declared that she would not be dancing for the ancestors, but for their notice. She was near enough to where I could dance toward her, lift my hands, and shake my wrist bells to the music.

"Focus, or we'll be placating *your* ancestors again," I said in an undertone. The woman was abashed, as her illness had been quite severe. She turned her attention to the patient and the words on the walls she could not read, but were familiar to her all the same.

My actions got me the approving nod from Tages.

Tages needed me to have my hands free. He was a Doctor-

Diviner, and supposedly would know what had caused her illness—but he was a scholar as well, and always wanted to gain as much information as he could get. The paint I'd put on the walls gave him more specific information to tailor those herbs for better healing Medicine.

The women danced, structured and free-form, to the beat. Each of us was given a chance to dance before the ill girl, and to dance to the ancestors symbolized by some of the markings on her arms and feet, as well as the walls. The minor doctors who danced, free-form, appealed to the ancestors for forgiveness of any perceived neglect—dancers who had successfully petitioned in their turn when they had suffered. Their success was necessary for the strength of the Medicine. With dance, music, chant, we all called upon the ancestors. Our music was loud, rhythmic, with even the bells and gourds and rattles adding to the rising of the beat of the drums that made the walls seem to sing with whispered words. Within this energy of the powerful Medicine, I took my turn to dance. This was trained and structured.

While the Medicine needed the spirits to be appeased, Tages loved science and good anatomy, and a clear diagnosis. With symbolic gestures, while I sang in Ndeb, I told Tages what was wrong with the girl.

Yes, she was cramping before her cycle, but her fever and the pain she felt were from her bladder. She could not urinate easily. The infection would only grow unless treated. I danced till I knew he had seen all I'd discovered while I'd examined her, and then stepped back to continue the structured dance of our drums and other musical instruments. I felt more breathless than usual, having felt Thefare's eyes on me as if I also wore a bodice that lifted my breasts to him.

36

Apprentice

At Tages's signal, Cai silenced the drumming to a slow beat, and the dancers stood back and swayed to his soft, steady rhythm. Now, everyone, thankfully, turned their gaze upon the Doctor-Diviner.

Tages spoke to the ancestors in Ndeb, which the spirits would know. It was filled with clicks and an odd mixture of consonants and vowels as musical and rhythmic as the music we'd just quieted. He chanted both ritual devices, as well as a list of instructions to me, as he mixed up the potion to go with the Medicine of music and the paint on the walls. He gave it to the girl and another sip to the mother. Both are bound in healing. The music started up again, and we danced to the ancestors, pleading for them to release her from pain.

When the fuss died down, I was set to clean the walls and bathe the girl again.

When it was a female concern, usually Velia took a more active part, instructing the patient with details that might prevent the illness from recurring. This time, she merely watched me work.

Tages was mildly surprised that Velia took a step back from her usual work, letting me take care of it. It was her right, and her craft. He seemed confused for a bit, but then left, pretty much leaving Cai and me to carry the heavy stuff. All of them left me to tend to the girl and handle the herbs and paint.

I took much of what Velia might have told the girl and talked to her about preventive measures. She was not sexually active, so she could not get a bladder infection that way if her husband entered her unclean. The cause was either food or her own lack of cleanliness after elimination. Some women's vulvas were built in such a way that contamination was easier than for others. Any particles of feces on the vulva could make a girl ill.

We spoke of food and of the body. Velia's instructions tended toward detailed frankness, so I did the same, even while embarrassing both Hastia and myself in the process. I was glad to move on to the potions and herbs that Tages had left behind.

I bid her to keep drinking the potion Tages had left behind. Having understood his instructions to me during his chant, I told her to drink plenty of fresh and clean water from a blessed white cup.

"I will," she said. "Thank you, Sen."

"You're welcome."

"Do you think this will also help me grow enough to marry?"

"I think your mother and Thefare are perhaps waiting for a proper match."

I could not quite tell her the truth. Though pretty enough, she was not beautiful. Her size and small breasts were not the only things that made her beauty questionable. She still had growing to do. The bones of her face were square, and her nose too wide. Awkward and coltish now, but later? I suspected beauty. Regardless, she was wealthy—and that would be a draw, especially in Thefare's lands.

"I've seen village women wed with breasts as small as mine. When they have a child, their breasts swell to make their child milk."

"Indeed," I said, for I knew it was true. Tages and Velia believed, however, that they'd been wed too early. The ritual of the Mother Tree was not performed when a girl first had her menses. It was performed when her breasts could support nursing a baby.

"I cannot wait for my turn to be blessed by the Mother

Tree!" Hastia said.

Yes, she was a girl who wanted the old ways. I could not say, "Me too!" I would not have my turn to become a full woman at a Mother Tree. My separation from my mother had been far more decided than the ceremony that made a young girl into a woman, blessed and included fully as a participating member of society. Grandmother Turani had given me life.

"You will no doubt soon have your ceremony," I said. "And be a woman."

The words had come out—and though I knew it to be true—it was not something I'd normally share. An apprentice Doctor-Diviner doesn't make proclamations or statements that might not occur. I should not *divine* her future, and it had sounded as if I had. I knew Hastia would be betrothed within the year. Something about it, however, troubled me. Still, I smiled at her, and then gathered up all my things and put them into my shoulder bag.

On the road, I thought back to what Thefare had said before the ceremony had begun.

Lord Thefare thought he knew who my parents were. Something in my features was recognizable, perhaps? Moreover, he believed he could ask Tages about it. While I had focused on the Medicine, I could not ignore the fact he had watched me dance quite speculatively. More, I thought Velia had seen it. I knew her speculative looks. How could that even matter, to either of them?

It had been the first time in my life I'd noted anyone looking at me with the same kind of speculation as Velia evaluating a new calf to keep or sell, or a cow if it were ready for to be cut up for stews, or even goods in the market she'd prefer to haggle over rather than buy outright.

Left to clean up the ceremony and walk home alone with

my bag full of my mask and other ceremonial accoutrements, I took time to consider this strange new thought. I realized that Thefare had implied some kind of claim on me. Thefare could not claim any authority over me. I'd been abandoned by my parents, for one, and I was now under the authority of Tages, who was my mentor.

I was stopped in my tracks, realizing that to someone like Thefare, my parents might matter more to him than my being an apprentice to Tages. It was a strange thought. I could only shake my head and remember that being Grandmother Turani's adopted daughter, or Tages's apprentice, were the only things that mattered to me. Could knowing my family of origin matter now?

Cai was right. I did not know the world outside Grandmother Turani's home. I had a feeling I would certainly learn!

Chapter Three

---«•»---

I came home to an intense discussion. I entered the gate of the enclosure and went toward the main round house where Tages and Velia were talking. I stopped on the threshold, wondering if I should go in. Velia wasn't angry, but her passion was elevated. I had been offered food as I'd left Arntlei's house, but I had refused, knowing what I would be given here.

I could smell the stew and the rich broth. Chicken this time, and rich with herbs. Velia simmered bones of any fowl we had eaten, with all the vegetable pairings from other meals, for at least three days. She'd simmer it till the bones were soft, and just before the broth smelled acrid, almost metallic—I had left it too long once—strain the lot, revealing a robust broth full of flavor. It made Arntlei's servant's broth look and taste like salted water with a chicken waved over it. I knew the stew's beans would be soft, as well as the leftover chicken meat. I could taste it in the very air, carried with the scent of curing herbs and the taste of curing cheese. I could see the one she'd opened for the household.

My mouth watered.

"You had the power of life and death in your hands once. Now what? Nothing? You betray it with this study of science... cutting down your worth and power," Velia was saying.

"You think that is what I am doing? You are wrong." There was a tone of pain in his voice. After a pause, he said, "If science can tell me a patient's needs better than divination, why is that a problem? Because I ask my apprentice to help me? She uses the Ndeb her guardian taught her, that I taught her."

"But women need the power of natural forces, divine power, and by accepting the call from Thefare, and not deferring to me, you cut down my power, like men who cut into a woman's Milk Tree to make liquor."

"They cut into wild trees, my dear," Tages said, "to power their own natural white fluids, as you well know." I could hear the grin in his voice. Yet when he spoke again, there was compassion. "I could not defy his request, and you seemed content to defer to my work."

"What else was I to do? And isn't that proof of why men are now in power, now beginning to own property their mothers would have given daughters? It robs women of their wealth. The cattle you saved being the only wealth they value, men value—but now they're taking away the homes once run by women."

Tages said something I could not catch.

"And he benefits from the trade his brother finds in his so-called exile. In my grandmother's time, even the men would have refused to let Fuluns return, or accept such tainted value to the community because of what he'd done."

"Are you suggesting that I control Thefare?" Tages asked, appalled.

"No, you're right. That's entirely foolish. I do ask that you stop science from diminishing what the ancestors or gods tell you. I ask that you stop teaching it to your apprentice. You will undermine her future worth. You've already betrayed our son by letting him study at the university."

"My dear, my role as a Doctor-Diviner is diminishing. Very few of us practice it with any kind of value."

She snorted and said, "Bathos," using that man's name like a curse.

Tages continued. "Science is taking over, regardless if you like it or not. Besides, at least in Sen's case, Turani was insistent that I train her."

"I will not stand for this! She will be lost to the changing world, and I hoped you would prevent it. Already she seems to lack the ability to speak to her own ancestors; isn't this going to make it harder?"

"I'm a good Doctor-Diviner. Even I cannot change the changing of this age. Our son might be proof of that, as he, too, lacks that skill." There was a pause, and he said in kinder tones, "You fight an endless battle. You must consider: What if science is a gift of the gods rather than proof of their diminishment?"

That was a statement I could ponder. What if it were a gift? What would it mean to me? I started to move into the light from the doorway, but I heard her speak again, and paused.

"Lord Aranthur has written again," Velia said. "Can you please answer him! He's offered rich patronage. Won't you accept?"

"You know why I can't," he said.

I could see them in opposition to each other. Velia was standing. Tages had his arms crossed, seated. Velia was pacing and gesturing with her hands as she implored. I stepped back.

"You are working less, Tages," she said.

"I worked a Medicine today," he said firmly.

"One person? In a waste of winter?" She waved the letter. "Lord Aranthur is distant enough, perhaps. If I accept that science has something to offer, and your learning of it, then..." She paused. I could hear the in-draw of a very deep breath. ". . . what you knew, and what you are now learning, can you not help him?"

He was silent.

I pondered what she'd said. However irritable she could be, Velia *could* think. She could expand her mind. I had learned quite a lot from her. I did understand her fears.

"Tages, you have lost our son to the university. I can understand. He has no gift, but plenty of your intelligence."

"We both gave him that!" Tages said emphatically.

"You gave him learning enough to enter it. Teach more than one apprentice. Put food on the table. We are losing Cai soon."

"We have food on the table," he countered.

"Because I put it there."

"I am content here, I must do the rites of testing with Sen. Then we shall see."

"She worked with Turani. I have hope she will meet your needs. Still, you have an adept who has long been ready for his Mastery, and an apprentice who is doing some adept work. Maybe helping Aranthur will give not only you a challenge but Cai and Sen as well!"

"He's a fool, Velia. He wants relics if he can get them, such as Thielle's broken necklace. His last overt attempt ended in disaster because of Fuluns's foolishness. More than that, his crime. He did no good to his brother, Aranthur, Rasce, or his daughter, Ravantha herself."

"Why not see if Thefare will finally sell it to him, now that Ati has a better?" Velia asked.

"Angling for it certainly hasn't put Aranthur on Thefare's good side, and the whole sordid fiasco cost Thefare a brother and rather valuable property, almost richer than all of his own. Aranthur doesn't, still, to realize that Thefare remains perturbed by it, damn his pride. I will not sour my own waters to help him. Besides, what Aranthur wants of me is magic, and I cannot do that."

"He says he is cursed, his family is cursed. Is that not what a Doctor-Diviner can cure?"

There was a strange pause. The energy of it crackled in the air.

"You know better than most why I cannot, right now. Besides, he wants a sorcerer. There are fewer of those, gods bless, than good Doctor-Diviners. Besides, Zelia *has* met with him in person. I trust her opinion. She is even better at diagnosis and divination than I am. There is no cure by placating the ancestors or other Medicine. Maybe science can save him? I doubt that. It is far too new. I certainly don't have enough science to diagnose him with it. He is desperate. Did you see the part in his letter where he wishes my aid in other ways? The man is a fool, and will die so. He will buy, or steal, every relic he can lay his hands on for healing that will never come," Tages said, sitting back down, folding his arms again.

"But Tages, the money! Even without that part." She shook her head and then scoffed. "Thieving Thefare. What is he thinking? But the healing; you must consider it," Velia said in a tone that always reminded me of grinding grains.

"It is moot, Velia. I am bound to Thefare, and under obligation to serve him and his people."

"But what if you could get out of that bond? Your sense of obligation? There's so much more that you could do, could learn!" she said.

I could tell by their poses, their stance, that this would take a while. I knew, especially with the placid look on Tages's face. I'd already eavesdropped far too much.

I considered the weather and the sky, and keeping to the shadows, moved back to the doorway. I quietly put my bag down beside the threshold and stepped away from the lit interior before they could notice me. Neither my bag nor I would suffer from the weather. It would rain in a day or two at most. Tonight was clear.

I went to sit under one of the trees inside the compound. I could still hear the discussion from one of the windows, but no longer any details.

"Survived the mountain lions?" Cai asked.

I started and looked up. He was resting on one of the sturdy branches of the tree.

"Obviously. It's not yet full dark, though." The path from the castle and compound was not the longest walk I'd made alone. Lions preferred to hunt at dawn. "I heard jackals in the hills, though, to the north."

I didn't tell him about the one I thought had been pacing me on my walk back. I couldn't be sure it was a jackal, to tell the truth. I never saw it with my eyes, only had the sense of Jackal's cackling laugh, and the sharp canine-like scent of it. If it had been nearby, however, it would have heard the pack and responded—like any other jackal might. The other pack had sounded close enough that the territory might be the same.

"I'll let Tages know," he said as I climbed up to join him.

Over the winter, I'd come to realize that my studies were different from those with which Cai was familiar. I was new to the household, and his apprenticeship had been with another master, so it had taken some moments to realize this. I could not tell if the difference was masters or some other kind of change.

From things Velia said and from his own account, as an apprentice, Tages had started to defy the often-haphazard training of his master by designing his own structured study of the Doctor-Diviner healing arts. His master chafed with a student so much greater than himself, and gave him his Mastery early, but sent him to rusticate in Thefare's lands, when Thefare was still a boy, and the landscape was still considered rich.

Tages once said, "I'd have been content to stay and study with him, but he didn't like it. I did not mind having him as a master as long as I could work on learning more."

He was a master of his art, but he always found a way to study more—even using his son's connections to gain more information. Long before that, he'd found Grandmother Turani, who taught him more Ndeb, with its rich lore of healing that was the underpinning of the language—something that even in his own apprenticeship had been fading. The lore had been tantalizingly close, but out of reach till he'd met and learned from her. This had naturally augmented the more ritualistic and symbolic side of his work, along with a vast lore of herbalism and physiology, giving a firm foundation to what we used now.

Still, he was a master around the same age as I was when I'd become his apprentice. Going from Grandmother Turani's herb lore to animal lore was not much of a leap, though he called upon a far more detailed study of the plants than she'd taught me, as well as animals. I, too, enjoyed the structured study of plants and animals founded upon the forest lore we loved.

Cai and I sat in the tree and watched the moon rise amid a chorus of lion roar from two different prides on either side of us. When he attained his Mastery, he had a living ready for him in his village.

Tages had learned the underlying science that ritual covered with what some might now call a veil of magic, or superstition. For the most part, over generations, peoples from islands south and west—the islands of Ster, or the greater island Dedathon—had brought their language to us. This was long before trade with the continental lands beyond them. Beyond their old gods and legends intermingling with ours, it was their languages intermingled with our own that had become Obrone.

Obrone was far more descriptive a language than Ndeb, in many ways. It certainly opened a greater and somewhat different study—or rather focus—of science. The studies, papers, and books in the city universities were in Obrone, and rarely in any of the dialects of the country. It opened up our understanding of the heavens and our world moving in it, as well as the medicinal parts of the sciences of chemistry, biology, and botany.

Tages, Cai, and I augmented Ndeb with Obrone when it came to details that the older language's mysticism kept secret. Ndeb was merely part of the deeper mysteries and traditions we valued.

There were, of course, Doctor-Diviners who used symbols, herbs, song, and dance completely at random, for display and showmanship, who believed far more in the power of magic than in the lore hidden in the ancient language. As taught to me by

Grandmother Turani, Ndeb was a working oral tradition long before universities started detailing on paper a growing body of knowledge. There was, I have to admit, a reason it was a dying language not spoken or understood fluently by Tages's colleagues.

My stomach growled, waking me up to the branch I was on.

Cai grinned. "Hungry?" I could see his teeth gleaming in the low light of near night.

I nodded.

"Why did Ati make a fuss about that necklace?" I asked.

"It is symbolic, I believe, of the broken necklace in Thefare's treasure room. It is said to have been made by Jammon himself, the gods' blacksmith and jeweler."

"Well, that's bound to impress some," I said. "How important do you think it was to the Medicine?" I had my own sense that it made no lasting impression.

He shrugged. "I couldn't tell you. Symbols are important to the dead as well as the living. Maybe more for the living."

"How so?"

"Think of Ndeb," he said. "There are more colors than white, red, or black. It is easier to use Obrone when dirty white, and blue is still considered a black."

"It's a language that roots us in the earth," I said, thinking of all the classifications of illness under red and black, and how often the plants used for it echoed those colors as well. "And azure, or Lapis, are gifts of nature, and well known in Ndeb."

"Yes. It goes from very general to highly specific, and little in between." He shrugged. "It's possible you, Tages, Zelia, and I are the last to speak it fluently," Cai said.

I shook my head. "Don't forget Aule. Still, that's a sad

statement on the role of the Doctor-Diviner," I said. My stomach growled again.

"I know. Unlike Bathos to the east. He's horrible," Cai said.

I laughed with him. "He doesn't even get the *herbs* right!" I said. "He just throws them together. Speaking of tradition, Hastia still wants a Mother Tree ritual."

"She's one of the few. Most consider the wedding to be when the child leaves her mother or family these days," he said.

"I don't really like that, though it obviously happens more often." It occurred to me that, as Velia was the person who often ran the Mother Tree rites for the young girls, she had reason to be more than peevish. "I like the ritual where the girl leaves her mother first, and becomes a woman, before becoming a bride. Too often, girls are getting married before their bodies are ready." And children carrying children in pregnancy also kept Velia busy, with their attendant complications. She feared for their lives, as she should. The change in this tradition was killing her patients.

"Velia said Aule is bringing some kind of tilling machine when he comes down next."

"Oh! For the new garden?"

"Yes, it is supposed to do more work than ten men."

"More time to study?" I said.

"Well, you don't mind Aule's machine coming over and cutting into the black earth, ripping into it like a man unbidden goes into a woman," Cai said roughly.

"That's an awful image."

"But it is true. It will dig into the land carelessly."

"Aule or I, no doubt, will be behind it—if not you. None of us is careless of the land," I said.

"Well, if this machine does what it says, she can't get you

to work for her as hard. You'll be out roaming the woods for more plants and animals for you and Tages to dissect."

"You're not?"

He grinned again. "You forget I'm to go back to my village soon. All the dead bodies are yours now."

He had a place waiting for him when he'd earned his Mastery. What did I have? The hurt was closer still. I said, "My closest friend, gone!"

"I have a girl back there I'll be wed to soon! I can't lament. Wed straight from her home, too," he said with a sigh. "No Mother Tree ritual for her."

"Does that bother you?" I asked.

"Yes. I've rather become accustomed to strong women who know their mind," he said with a grin. "But she's a good girl, and it's been planned for a long while. We've been corresponding lately through a scribe. She seems as if she's become a strong woman. I know she's beautiful."

My stomach growled again. "Meyelia is her name, right?" I asked.

He looked, to my surprise, a bit bashful. "Yes."

"I'm happy for you. It's a few days' walk to your village if I remember. Your village is west of here, in Rasce's lands?"

The moon had risen, and it was nearly full. We heard the huffing roar of a lion to the north, carried in the bright, clear night.

"Yes, I'm west, almost due west, past the lord-locked Westvell," he said and shivered.

Why did Cai shiver at the sound of lions? We were used to night noises like this, as Tages had his home away from any village— he did not like being disturbed at random for common ailments.

"It's just lions," I said. A lion from a pride to the southwest huffed and roared in response to the first.

"Yes, but the Westvell is claimed by Lady Ravantha. She stands between her father and Thefare." He grinned at me. "You really don't pay attention to any of the nobility around here, do you?"

"Maybe my head's been in books too long, or out in the woods," I said, but thought of some of what I'd just overheard.

"Sen, you have to pay attention to this," he said.

"A woman holding the lands now usually kept by men? Surprising in this day and age. Who is her husband? A Westvell?"

Cai shrugged. "No, she's not married. The name isn't for family land, and she's certainly not adopted the name for her own as the lords of the land do. I gathered she was to wed Lord Aranthur's son, Marce, I think it was. Their land is beyond that of Rascenden. But something happened. That was about eighteen, twenty years ago or so. Might be less. I don't know all the history, but I was told some of it because I had to travel through the Westvell."

"Such as?"

"Rasce was negotiating some deal with Thefare for land that came to Ravantha when her grandmother died. It would not serve Aranthur, as it was locked by two opposing lords, and far from the land she would rule with her husband."

"And the deal went awry?" I asked, having had a hint of it earlier.

"Clearly. She guards her land with a vicious hand. Even her father is no longer welcome to traverse without permission into the lands once held as a dower house for his mother."

"How did you traverse the Westvell to get here?"

"I was a boy and guided by Tages. No one bothers Tages."

"True. If he doesn't escort you back, maybe Velia and I can escort you home?"

Cai snorted. "She won't go. She only goes on trips to see Aule and find out the latest fashion."

"I'll talk to Tages."

"You'd have to walk back alone then, with not only a threat from mountain lions and jackals and snakes and so on... but an angry female."

I shook my head. "And even you say you've gotten used to a strong woman! If Ravantha's father let her have the property, clearly it was with reason."

He laughed. "You have a point there. And I'm leaving you to it, probably around the time Aule comes home with his newfangled invention! Maybe it will finally plow a furrow between them that would make her go back to find her own place."

I shook my head. The sounds of discussion had changed. It had gotten somewhat quiet, but we both knew what would soon ensue.

"I may have to sleep in this tree tonight." I gestured to the main round house. "And I haven't eaten."

"You could join me in my hut," Cai offered.

I chuckled. "No, thank you!"

He did not take it personally. "But come down. I did save you some food. I forgot. Sleep in the tree if you prefer," he said as he scrabbled down. "Unless you change your mind."

I laughed. "No, Cai. Go to bed. But the food first."

I went back down and got the bowl of cold stew he'd saved for me. I ate, looking at the stars, finding contentment. After a while, I climbed back into the tree and settled onto the branch.

The lions would roar throughout the night, ensuring that the other pride knew where it was, in a verbal show of marking territory.

I thought back to that morning, and the memories of the cold that had broken a branch and let it weep into my hand with the warmth of day. I thought about change.

Sometime after my arrival, Aule had seen one of my first journals and taken it with him. He'd left to study at one of the great god cities, Jambrone, near the headwaters of the great lake that some called an inland sea.

He'd wanted to read some of my early notes where I had compared the ancient Ndeb means of classification with the new, university-defined taxonomy we'd found in one of the books Tages, Aule, and I had read. The book had inspired Aule's departure. We'd all found it intriguing. My drawings of a couple of plants and animals and subsequent discussion—at that point written in Obrone—went alongside a written version of Ndeb I was attempting to create, trying to reconcile two seemingly divergent paths of study.

He was intrigued by my attempt to write Ndeb. The books brought the idea of scholarship to another level. Before he left, our studies exploded with industry. At the time, in these notes, I had only been hypothesizing that Ndeb had an underlying system of classification, trying to see if there was enough information for further comparison and study.

If I had no future home, no future role in which to step, as Cai did... what if I explored this idea further?

The system of colors in Ndeb has only three primary terms: white, red, and black, barring terms of distinct colors from specific minerals, rocks, or even beetle parts. Azure. Carmine. Saffron. Other words of color were metaphorical phrases, such as the specific green "Oil of the Olive" or the yellow "like beeswax" or orange, ritually equivalent to red.

The original language and healing system had developed before international trade.

There was, I understood, a white berry from Yezgin that, when roasted, turned red. It supposedly had healing properties—amid quite fantastical legends of mythic life extension. White, it was just a berry; red, it became something else.

This alone would have been a great plant for Ndeb healing—except for the incongruous white-to-red transformation. It added to this potential study, the intrigue of it all, and what classifications in Ndeb could echo in modern, university-based plant taxonomies.

Therapeutic importance in Medicine was—obviously—good, and within the sense of whiteness was strength, life, making visible, sweeping clean, and washing, along with prosperity and freedom from misfortune. The state of health, spiritually and physically, is white. Clean. Pure. It was why the Mother Tree ritual had once been so important—with the tree's white sap representing milk, or, less often, semen, also quite important for generating life.

Red is power, such as the strength and joy one gets in eating flesh—its blood being red—and strengthening. It's also the blood that binds mother to child. It's a complicated color because it can also show ill health, such as blood in the urine, or a person becoming yellow with jaundice. *Red* where red ought not to be. It can reveal illness.

Black goes beyond blue and other dark colors. In positive tones, it was akin to rich soil that fed plants with subtle power, or power as rooted as the strongest trees—but unseen. Known, yes, but not seen, as few can see the roots of a tree till it falls. In negative tones, it is a lack of luck, suffering, misfortune, and *what is secret*—decidedly an indication of illness.

To reach to the positive side of this is why a Doctor-Diviner's healing Medicine includes not only divination to reveal secret causes of illness or arguments and other strife, but also includes minor doctors—that is, community—to help augment not only an appeal to ancestors, but to support the person who was ill in gaining pure, clean health. What is secret—and therefore diseased—is revealed. This happened through divination. It was why healing was often a group effort, even if the Doctor-Diviner provided the Medicine. Especially when the illness was more social, and we were mediating the illness of strife in a community.

To combat illness, great Medicine included the community, including ancestors, with dance and song, as well as healing herbs and extracts. The afflicted were always supported by people who could empathize and support the one who was suffering. It could not be hidden, even if we gave it as much respect as possible.

As Doctor-Diviners, we removed those things that made people or a community ill. It was part of our role, even if rarely seen in recent years or even recent generations.

I doubted Bathos, for instance, had mediated any community through a conflict. Among the first things I'd seen Tages do was just such a thing, when the wells in the poor side of the village were sickened by being too close to untended waste. Tages not only navigated the cause of the illness, refusing to blame the poor, and put the blame squarely on one of Thefare's foremen of the area who hadn't paid enough attention, or care, to what might have poisoned more water sources and more wells—a sickness within a community, and the conflicts of blame and responsibilities all managed by Tages, Doctor-Diviner.

Yes, people did die, but the community came together for it, and those who were responsible for mismanaging the water systems of the poor community were made to fix the problem. The illness could have spread from the poor communities and upward to even Thefare's perch, where no natural water could be found, with him living on top of a rock.

Bathos could barely navigate his own garden, much less the woods and fields around his village. While I had already far more knowledge and use of it than he had, he'd been given the scars of our office. I had none. He missed entirely the rich woven tapestry of nature, humans, and the Divine—our lives from birth to death, interwoven and interconnected with the living and the ancestors. Thus, it was impossible for him to do more than to perform mumbo jumbo, pull some of those strings at random, even if he happened to notice them.

Many of those metaphorical colors describing either plants or body parts—including internal body parts—revealed a rather elaborate classification system nearly lost in the hokum practiced by some in the country. At some point, an oral tradition of a language will break down as it becomes supplanted by a different one. I wanted to use what I'd learned from Grandmother Turani to compare Ndeb with the more modern and accepted taxonomy we had read in the books Tages had bought, and Aule was learning.

I had been writing the idea down and crafting a possible defense for Tages, so I could support future adept-level study.

I'd discussed this, tentatively, with Aule before he left as a field of study for me to pursue, not having formed my idea fully. I had hoped the conversation would bring clarity and more books that might aid my research. I knew Aule had his own interests he wished to pursue—chemistry, and the deeper qualities derived from herbs, such as minerals and more. He wanted to know how to extract them better, but more than that, to understand how these elements created such wondrous things in our world.

Aule, after he'd settled in, had given my pages to one of the professors who taught botany, a Professor Cuintus. The professor kept the pages; in fact, he had been impressed enough to frame the pictures, and apparently used them in his teaching. Cuintus sent me a better book on the taxonomy of plants around the Great Lake, along with other books to further my studies—not yet realizing I was female.

Aule came through with other books, sharing more than botany, in his chosen field. Chemistry had terms that were as strange as a new language.

As I listened to the lions roar, and the stars spilled out into the black sky, I began to plan how I could now truly turn what I was learning into a focused study and book. I could study till Grandmother Turani's destiny for me unveiled itself the way night unveiled the stars.

Chapter Four

‹‹•›››

T ages allowed me to escort Cai through the Westvell. Cai had a spring in his step. He had his master's scar on his right hand, and more white clay to help it heal clean and white. The scar being on the dominant hand was important, as it would require a time of reflection for it to heal properly. It also required a new master of our art to know how to heal wounds more quickly and cleanly.

I was happy to celebrate with him, as far as walking him back to his home. I would miss him. He was good with people. Excepting people like Kutu, I was not, having been raised in near solitude in Grandmother Turani's woodland grotto.

We'd been surrounded by the bounty of nature. She spoke as if they were all old friends, and to some degree, they were mine, as well.

"Spirits of living nature," she'd once said, "are as important as the Divine. Gods are often bound to the ideas of those who worship—the spirit of *ideas*, you could say—for people define us...

that is... *them*." She'd sighed at her mistake. It had been something I'd been noticing, this shifting of pronouns as she aged. "Thielle's temple in Jambrone is no longer where maidens rise up the hidden steps to reach into the heavens to draw down the... cosmic glue of love and harmony. No, the temple is now a place where women ply their wares on their backs with open legs or open mouths."

"Grandmother!" I'd said in shock.

"Well, it's true. Thielle is just an old woman living in a forgotten grotto, missing her twin."

"Like you, living in a grotto with an adopted daughter?" I asked gently.

She'd turned to me and smiled—but I couldn't read her smile. It seemed to say so many things, mocking like Crow or Jackal.

"Spirit of *ideas*, Sen. The old gods are dying. New ones must rise. I will go to Nhor's Ugly Grotto someday." Granted, she sometimes would say, "I will go to my sister's grotto one day." Nhor was a goddess of the dead. It was clear to me that she knew she was dying. An old friend had come to guide her. I hadn't even known. Clearly, she hadn't wanted me with her.

Those thoughts had turned upon a coin, and she began to talk to the trees and nature, guiding me again toward them. She'd laugh when I said I thought Jackal mocked me. Still, besides Kutu, in some way, they were my few friends. I hadn't met a great many people during my life with her. They were people who were desperate for healing and thought "Old Mother Love" would give better—or cheaper—healing than Zelia or Tages.

Cai's life had been far more social, with interactions far less philosophical, mystical, or theological. I'd envied that.

Apprentice

I'd seen him calm a crying child as he poulticed the boy's myriad burning ant bites, or make a little girl have a crush on him, just because he gently cleaned a scrape on her knee. Mothers tended to fall for him, as well as a number of single women. I had some idea he made use of this, but no confirmation of that. I'd trust him with any Medicine. He certainly trusted Velia's women's medicines and magic. I would not trust him with a pretty young woman, unless she knew her mind.

I was glad for him, though the bounce in *my* step had less to do with any happiness for him. I'd already tilled the field in the earliest dawn hours as best I could without Aule's machine. We had left with the serenade of spring—birdsong, and Velia singing to the gods and nature spirits before planting seeds. It started to rain an hour outside Thefartown. We stopped to cover his fresh Mastery scar on his hand. He thought that it was best not to get it too wet. Halfway into the day's journey, despite the steady, soft rain that had silenced the birds' morning salute, I realized that I felt free.

Tages had not let me go without a task, however. I was to gather spring plants that did not grow within an easy distance of his small compound. The first night, Cai and I were given a place to sleep in a village where he used both ritual and herb to cure an earache and headache in a man.

Cai had not brought any herbs with him, excepting the seeds and rootstocks he would use to grow his own medicinal garden. With his healing hand, I would have to be his hands, so we went out to forage. We quickly noted that some Monkey Orange was close at hand. "Yellow fruit" that came from greenish white flowers, which was "bitter and strong."

Many people called it a Monkey Orange—proof of Obrone's

international etymology. There are no monkeys native to our country, and the fruit of this tree was not at all like the citrus fruit that had its cultivar origins on the continent far to the south in countries with exotic names like Bouyask and Yezgin.

When I first came to study with Tages, he had taken me on one of his now-rare visits to the coast. I learned later it was to assess how I would handle new experiences and a wide variety of people. Far better than books, that trip exposed me to the possibilities of a larger world. For Tages's purposes, he noted the seeds of my passion for knowledge beginning to grow. To celebrate, he bought us oranges. They were juicy, sweet, with a bit of tang—but tasted like possibilities and joy. We saved the rinds for Velia.

All the other oranges he brought back on his now rare trips were insipid. Age made the interior less juicy, but as long as the rinds were still somewhat plump, Velia would have me carefully slice off the zest for her. Tages would use some, as well, to help the flavor of some of his concoctions. Throughout the months, the rind would come into some part of a meal and remind me of a larger world and that there was so much more to learn.

Monkey Orange did not have a fruit that was juicy or particularly sweet. It was certainly not a treat.

This "orange" was good for several different purposes, from increasing milk for lactating women and curing venereal disease to increasing strength. In Ndeb, one of the phrases considered it a "strong tree," which is why its craftsmen often used it for woodwork.

Through the university's taxonomy—along with my understanding of the tree through Ndeb—I knew the tree to be useful for improving cardiovascular blood flow as well as an analgesic, among other things. I'd known it to be useful for headaches, as did Cai.

I gathered bark and flowers and gave them to Cai. He exercised his Mastery and brewed the infusion while otherwise working on healing the patient. I drew the flowers and leaves, as well as pressing the flowers and leaves for Tages to see, noting its location. We had some people often coming to us, including a messenger from the Westvell interested in cures for headache. Tages would be glad to know that there was some Monkey Orange nearby, if he didn't know or divine it already.

On the second day, late afternoon, after taking a slight detour, we walked to Grandmother Turani's home, built against some low boulders. The entryway to the Women's Compound was similar in technique; those boulders had been brought to the compound. This house was built with the boulders where nature had laid them.

On one side wall, bricks closed a hollow between two massive stones. That hollow, on the inside, had been part of my bedchamber. More walls were built on the sides of some of the boulders of the house, making it large and roomy. One room, my favorite, used a huge boulder atop three others to create a cool room on the inside, with a doorway and walls that bricked up the gaps with such tight seams as to make some houses in Thefare's seem poor copies. The house had always been a strange, winding place with odd nooks and crannies. Grandmother Turani's house went deep between various boulders in the cavern-like house, so many of the rooms were still lit with the glow of light from outside, guarded by a hedge of old, espaliered acacia trees that enclosed the herb garden. I knew I would have to come back. The garden was woefully overgrown, and the fence needed trimming.

Cai had never seen such work up close and was amazed at how well structure and nature combined. There were no gaps between the carved brickwork and the boulders.

"Thefare would give his back teeth for the main gate to the Women's Compound to be so well done!" he said.

"The art, I gather, has long since been lost."

There were stone lintels that held up more stonework, and sometimes created doorways in larger walls. Technically, it was mine now. My home, if I were ever to choose to use it. Would people venture far for just me? They came for Grandmother Turani. She said that her little grotto had once been an ancient temple to Thielle, or part of one. There were worn, stair-like depressions in the largest boulder, leading up to what might once have housed a temple of sorts. Stairs to rise up to the heavens, to reach the *stuff* that could help one weave harmony into a community, into one's soul. People came to Turani out of nearly lost tradition, habit, for her well-earned reputation as a healer. They came sick, sick of body, sick of heart, and left happier and healed.

Would they come for an untried Master Doctor-Diviner, the unproven heir to Turani's or Tages's skill?

"That's old stonework," Cai said. "But there are some amazing modern structures you'll find uniquely beautiful and well-made, once we get past the Westvell. They are even better than Thefare's manor. He's a poor lord compared to Rasce or Aranthur, whose lands are rich from grain."

I thought a moment, thinking of the fight the night of Hastia's Medicine. "Aranthur's land, Aranthenden, is beyond, correct?"

"Yes. Come on, let's keep going," Cai said.

"Do you not want to stop here for the night?"

"There's enough daylight, and I'd like to get home. Let's see you show off your hunter skills, and I'll show off some of mine." He flexed his shoulders to shrug off his shoulder bag. His pack might not have healing herbs, but it did have his small bow, as well as fishing line and snares.

I laughed, but that night we slept in the open air, building a wall of thorn branches to keep ourselves safe, like hunters did. The acacia needles were long and sharp, but the scent made us feel as if we were guarded by the smell of warm honey and a floral, yet freshly wet-earth scent.

"I'm glad that Kutu showed you how to wrestle with these things," Cai said the first night, nursing a scratch. He turned some of his hunt on a stick. The herbs I carried helped to flavor the bird.

"He knew I travel alone at times to hunt plants."

"He likes you."

I shook my head. "I just happened to find him moments after he was bitten by a snake. He was grateful."

"No, he likes you," he teased. "He brings you food and tells you stories about different animals, the secret Hunter folklore! He'd like to marry you, I think, when you're free."

"A lot you know. He's already married and has a growing brood of children. He's merely glad I saved him from a rather painful death. Those snares you use came from him, so why tease me about it?"

I fussed over the food for a moment, then asked, "What was it about the mushrooms he had for Tages?"

"Pardon?"

"When we were gathering clay. Or I was. You were getting rabbits."

"Well, Velia did want me to tell you about it. It's a special mushroom some Doctor-Diviners use for their own Medicine work."

"How?" I asked.

"Tages says that other shamans in other countries have similar journeys. It opens their perceptions."

"We're going somewhere for my initiatory adept test?" I asked.

He shook his head. "Yes and no. It's a journey into the spirit world, where we climb the boughs of the spirit tree and look to the other side. A Milk Tree type of ceremony.

"The Milk Tree ceremony is an initiation from girl to woman."

"This is also a kind of initiation, but specifically for shamans and Doctor-Diviners. You will see the spirits of your dead, and they will guide you."

Is it frightening? I wondered. I thought of Nhor, who was a goddess of the dead, who was supposedly more frightening than what you might find on the other side.

He shook his head again. "To be able to divine, you must be able to read runes, but you can often learn more when you dream of the dead. This will help you do that." He stopped walking and looked at me. "Unless you don't want to be a Doctor-Diviner."

"I do!" I said.

"Then expect whatever happens, it will be quite strange, but... worth it. Now, let me quiz you. An easier test than that. What does your precious Ndeb say of this plant?" he asked, nursing another scratch.

"There are a lot of uses," I said, taking some of the sap and putting it on his scratches. "Much of what I know, however, is not from this region. The books I've read from Aule say that the species is even more abundant in lands to the south and is more robust. They use the bark to make decoctions after the tree is seven years old and the bark has cured for at least a year. The gum is used to make those confections. Thefare's cook hates to make them, and Aule tells me he does badly anyway. Do you remember Old Man Visnai?"

"Yeah. The man with the teeth problems."

"The gum Tages used was acacia."

"I don't remember him gathering it, and I know I haven't, nor you. How does he get it?"

"He doesn't. He gets it from the hunters who cut the trees for overnight fencing," I said, with a wave to ours, "when they move small herds of cattle from one village to another to improve stock with either exchanges or breeding." I pointed out where I'd set a pot to gather the slow-seeping sap.

Cai laughed. "I knew the man was smart."

I grinned at him as well.

Cai had chosen not to follow the road, claiming that I was handy enough with the acacia fences. It would cut our travel time, as there was a wide curve away from this somewhat forested area, though close to a few villages. After we left the cattle country, the land grew even more wild. It was not densely forested, and certainly had moments of grassland. Travel was not hard, but at times inconvenient with the number of thorn bushes scattered among the grasslands. We were heading toward more trees.

The following afternoon, we came across some old ruins. The structure had been built on a far more elaborate scale than Grandmother Turani's house. Great walls were built with pale bricks and with huge boulders. Old lichen of pale greens and some deep oranges made elaborate patterns against the dark granite. It shamed the old structures of the Women's Compound, displaying what greatness they could have been. Nature had encroached, showing that the cattle plains had once been verdant with dense forest growth. We had never come across ruins quite like this.

"Look at that. It's hard to believe that Thefare and even Rasce's lands were like this," Cai said. "You don't think about it when you are in the forests like this, to think about how different it might have been. Seeing this place, overgrown like it is."

"To see it, after reading about it, is quite surprising."

"You read about this?"

"Not this," I said, waving at the ruins. "You know that old book Tages has about the history of this area?"

"Oh, yeah. I never read it. It wasn't about healing. It looked boring."

"It is. And not exactly interesting to a healer. I was reading it to try and help me fall asleep! One of the things I noticed was how, generations ago, they listed how many acres they cleared. I think that they must have built in wood at some point, but after a time, if you clear all the trees, what do you get?"

"Rolling hills with scrub trees, thorn trees, bushes, and plenty of underbrush for cattle to eat. They like to eat bark, too. So that doesn't help."

"But places like this are no longer on cattle trails," I said.

Cai nodded. "This place must be ancient."

At the top of the hill, we explored like curious children. We came across what must have been an enclosed garden, with fruit trees that showed how, in nature, they might have been under canopy trees with other trees towering over them on the other side of a disintegrating wall. There was even one lone hardy olive, and not one of the wild ones with hard and nearly useless fruit. There were plenty of suckers sprouting at its base, and tiny trees at its feet.

"These won't have a chance to thrive here," I said.

"Not with other competing plants!" he said. "Acacia will try to dominate, given the chance." He gestured toward part of the grasslands. From the vantage, a few days or a spare two weeks earlier, we could see an encroaching carpet of budding light green canopy to the south. The white flowers were gone, and the whistling of the trees came thin without their fragrance.

I dug up one of the small olive trees. "Velia will like it," I said. "If I can keep it safe on the trip, anyway."

Cai laughed when I dug up a second one. "And here's one for you to placate your wife and show her that you intend a long and happy future for you and your family together."

He accepted the gift. "Thank you, Sen!"

We continued to explore to the top of the ruins, built upon a hill of stone, as if under all the exposed boulders and hiding dirt, there must have been one huge mound of granite rising above the land. As Cai was exploring nearby, I thought to myself that it must have once dominated the land, giving view to the whole landscape for miles. Had there been fewer trees, we would have seen rolling mountains and hills and outcroppings of granite that might have been mountains. I looked about, moving deeper into the ruins, past stone and brick walls to find three lone chimneys.

Cai refused to join me. "That's an old temple," he said, moving away.

I looked at him in some confusion. All his enthusiastic exploring had suddenly evaporated. He did not seem spooked, however, just bored.

"It's beautiful," I said. There was a huge tree full of white buds, and some flowers in full bloom. It twisted up from the floor space in the middle of the chimneys.

"It's just an old ruin, Sen."

"What of the tree?"

"Seen one tree and you've seen them all!"

I was surprised by this. He had been as eager as I had been to see what grew here and had even followed suit to my digging for an olive sucker, to gather up other orchard saplings, including apple, to give to his future bride. And this tree I was looking at was also budding with promise of being something unusual—just the type of tree I had been tasked to find, draw, and describe to our mentor. I realized, watching him, that somehow Cai did not even *see* this tree. His eyes moved past it as if all he saw was the vista below, past the chimneys.

There had been times, I had come to realize, since last winter, that I did sometimes see things that Cai did not, and I believed Tages did not as well, astute as he was with divining.

His face almost blank, Cai turned away and said, "Come on. I've got to get to my future wife. And we still must get through the Westvell," he said.

"I'll stop back here then, on my way home."

But I lingered. Looking at the tree, I felt a hint of melody and Grandmother Turani's arms. I went to the tree and touched it, realizing that the vague song was the lullaby that Turani used to sing to me. I still could not remember all the words, but another line came into my mind:

"One was wrapped
In lace and gold
Another leaves and dirt

70

Apprentice

One died in the cold
The other death did skirt

Oh, the humble child
Into my arms did come..."

As if on a breeze, I heard something I could only translate as "And she will be something more." Other rhyming words, like drum and thumb and even bum, tried to interfere, tried to create the next few lines. Some words came that seemed more and more absurd to the seeming tone of the song, and increasingly less likely. More than that, I knew I was missing something within the second stanza. I didn't remember that surprising line from the lullaby, but it seemed to be part of it, somehow. I shook my head, trying to think of where that might be in the poorly remembered song.

All I knew now was that there had been something said about three chimneys and a destiny. Not in the song, but somehow the image was strong. I was the humble child. In all my wanderings, I had never been here, and yet...

"This is where she found me," I said. It felt like a memory, but one I could not have had, being a baby.

There was more, as well. I could see the claw marks on the tree and realized that one side of the tree was healthy and blooming, but there was the beginning of damage. Ants were already climbing up and through in places. This reminded me of something Grandmother Turani had once said—beyond the lullaby, I could not remember. About a tree that was clawed by lions, who frightened the birds away, and it rotted and was gnawed beneath. She'd sent me to study with Tages, having said something that had driven my need to learn. "There's only so long you must study, and you must learn so much! You must bind the two that had been divided by one—bind the three together before the Tree dies."

It had not made sense. Looking at what must be the Tree, I still did not understand. What was I supposed to?

By then, she was forgetting things and confusing many things and many stories about people I did actually know. A story about Kutu would be confused with Tages. A lion in a story would do jackal-like things, and the story itself might be out of order. She wasn't sure how to dress herself some days. There were times she wasn't sure how to make tea, if the water ought to be hot or cold to brew, much less how to make it hot if that was necessary.

If she gave me a destiny at that time, a purpose or quest—it wasn't, perhaps, reliable.

Tages had warned me of her growing senility during one of his visits. She'd been angered by this, grumbling as if it were some kind of accusation of mental illness. But she was mercurial then, and she'd also muttered, "Well, I shouldn't be offended. Even gods get old, I suppose."

I had clung to the times of reason, or rather, merely familiar. There were increasing times when I could not at all understand what she'd meant. Tages coming to fetch me by her plans had been heartbreaking, but also a relief. The burden of caring for such a beloved, yet unpredictable soul had been heavier than I'd realized. He'd promised she was safe. "A friend of hers came to let me know they were escorting her to her sister's home."

"Who?" I asked.

"I don't know if you've met her, but Tai?"

I had. She also went by Kuen-Tai. She had visited rarely, but memorably. An odd woman, tall and lithe, golden, almost amber skin, and almond eyes, always in white and red. Her strange, lurid tattoo, blazing carmine as bright and red as that made from the far southern cochineal beetle, as distant as she herself was. I trusted her. It was as if she carried calmness with her like a scent.

When she was there, Grandmother Turani's spinning, random, and strange thoughts seemed to come to a still and centered place. She was herself again. I still didn't know if Turani was alive or dead, but considering her age, I assumed the latter.

I shook myself again, away from memories, away from the song.

Cai had already started climbing down the hill. I found stairs between old boulders, with old stepping-stones fitted neatly into the massive stone walls around me. "I'll come back," I said to the stones and the Tree. A riot of birdsong seemed to answer me from above. And one lone crow made that eerie spring caw. I looked up to see it in one of the dead or dying branches.

We joined the road a few hours later. As soon as we did, Cai's mood improved. The contrast was marked. One moment we'd been exploring rather cheerfully—he could never have been Tages's student without a sense of curiosity—the next, his whole demeanor was flat. Now he told me tales about his family, laughing at his brothers' misdeeds, which told me his rather robust attitude toward sex was probably a family trait. It was a wonder Cai hadn't gotten himself in as deep trouble as they had, but Thefarland had too many echoes of a woman's focused attitude toward physical relations and relationships, at least among the general populace, to make any children less of an issue. Besides, Cai knew the many ways of preventing pregnancy a well-rounded healer ought to know, especially as pertains to the health of women. He had Velia to thank for that, even without Tages.

I let him prattle on and pondered the strange shifts, wondering at the Tree he had not seen. It was the first time I had known that I did see things he could not—something Tages had also commented on a time or two. The realization that he'd been hinting that I could see things that even he did not was surprising. It was not something I could ask Cai about. He might think me mad. And yet, how could I know what Cai could see or not see, that I could and he could not? I could not borrow his eyes, any more than he could mine. If he had not seen it, was the Tree even real?

Chapter Five

———— «‹•›» ————

I felt as if I knew when we walked across the boundaries into the Westvell. I felt watched throughout the day. One moment we were merely walking along the road, and then the next... it was akin to that *predator-nearby* feeling well known to both of us.

A few minutes later, Cai confirmed it. "We're in her lands."

"I know; I feel watched," I said.

Cai was deeply disturbed by this; his mood changed once again, and this time with far more reason. It felt as if we were walking slower, our feet unable to match the beating of our hearts.

"It's said that she has spirits of women guarding her lands," he said. "I'm glad you're here."

We were miles into the land when a woman in her thirties, dressed like a man, stepped forward. She had the classic men's cloak, and if leggings hadn't been invented, she would probably have sported the loose spring outfit that revealed a man's legs. Modern leggings and a man's traditional spring cloak were not as incongruous as I might have thought, having seen Thefare in a far more garish blending of old and modern styles.

Like any initiated hunter, she wore both a bow, with its quiver full of slender, well-fletched arrows, and a sword. When she moved, I saw a bodice under her cloak, tight to her body, but built more like a man's formal vest than any bodice Ati might have worn to show off her cleavage to her husband and all the world. This revealed nothing, with looser fabric going over the shoulders, and only a hint of chest below the neck. I considered that, athletic as she was, this bodice probably prevented the painful bouncing of full breasts that running might otherwise entail. It looked more comfortable than bands of cloth tied around my chest when I did harder gardening work.

"What is your purpose here?" she asked.

I stepped forward before Cai could speak. "I am Sen of the Woods; we are traveling through the Westvell to his home." Cai showed off his scarred hand.

She raised an eyebrow. "Interesting that you thought of a woman escorting a man through these lands. How did you come to such an idea?"

"He is a new master, trained by the Doctor-Diviner Tages, who is also my master," I said, deflecting the question. "We are looking for plants we might find on the way to Rascenden that we might not find nearer our home."

She looked at us both thoughtfully, gazing at me a long while. She came forward and reached up to my face. I tried not to flinch as she lifted my chin and ran her fingers through my hair with the other hand.

Men—including the hunter Kutu, as well as Cai—had, at times, looked at me as if they wished to possess me or bed me. Her gaze and touch were not overtly sexual, but I had never felt such desire to possess me or own me as what I felt from this woman.

Even if he did not understand it, I knew that I was not alone in such a sense. Cai's shoulders bowed up, and his stance shifted as if squaring off against a rival.

"I could almost name you," she said.

"She just gave you her name," said Cai.

She glared at him. To me, she said, "I mean, I can guess who your parents are."

This again? I thought.

"And who are you?" Cai asked.

She glared back at him for a moment. "I am Ravantha, sometimes called Ravantha Malavish, Lady of this land."

Poor Cai went pale and stepped back, his shoulders dropping. She chuckled.

"You have not spoiled this lass on your travels here?" she asked. Her voice gentle, but her eyes cruel.

"I cannot," he said. "I am to wed," he added, but I could hear the words fall flat.

"Velia is your local healing woman, married to Tages?" Ravantha asked.

"Yes," he said.

She laughed again and turned back to me. I did not like her attention any more than Cai did, though it had a different energy, more like passion than loathing.

"For the herbs Tages sends me on a regular basis, I will let him pass, if you promise to come speak with me when he is safely through."

"Or?"

She leaned down and whispered in my ear. I will not repeat

what she said, but I could not let her do that to Cai.

"I will meet with you on my return journey."

I refused to use the polite *my lady* with her. I did not want to be connected with her in any way. She looked too hungry. She had threatened my friend, and I was uncomfortable that she viewed me as something like prey.

We walked past her as calmly as we could, but as soon as we were out of sight, we both broke into a run. When we stopped, I was weeping. Though we were both breathless from our run, I was also choking with pent-up fury.

"What are *you* so mad about?" Cai asked. "She was ready to cut my manhood off."

I shook my head. She was not planning on that, I knew. But the humiliation would have been equal, I thought.

"Twice in this month, two people said they knew who my parents were!"

"Oh," he said. "Wouldn't you want to know?"

"In part, and yet... why should I? They left me to die of exposure. It wasn't even neglect that we've sometimes seen in new, but depressed, mothers. They left me to die a slow death of dehydration and starvation, and whatever else the elements had to offer. Even if it were spring, as a baby, I could easily have drowned in a downpour."

Cai looked abashed. "I hadn't ever thought of it like that," he admitted.

I shook my head. "Exposure is a cruel, hateful death for a child. The parents walk away from a baby's lonely cries and never worry at the suffering it might feel. Maybe they thought a predator would make short work of it, ripping it apart before it starved."

"That's awful, Sen!"

How could I not expect to feel deep resentment for the parents who had left me to die? Had not wanted me. "What does it matter who my parents were, except to know I cannot value them? I believe the ancestors or gods have already meted out their punishment, so I don't even need to think of any revenge. My mother and father were Grandmother Turani, and she loved me with all her heart. I never even thought about any other parents till the other day! So, what does it matter to either Thefare or to Ravantha? Who am I to *them*?"

I could only take comfort in the truth that I was apprentice to Tages and Grandmother Turani's adopted child.

"Do you want my thoughts as a young Master Doctor-Diviner?" he said.

"Sure."

"I think it all needs to get out into the open, so it can heal."

"You think I'm hurt by this?"

"Obviously, because their feelings on the matter have a great impact on their thinking and involve you."

I looked over at him. This was one of the things I admired about Cai. He did have insight. I could see he had more to say.

"Their thoughts are like an illness and need to be confronted. Now, how would I do that if I were to heal it? I can't tell you. Tages could."

I sighed. "I'll trust him, as always."

"Yes." He gripped my shoulder. "Come on, let's get this trip over with," Cai said.

"Gladly."

"But you have to go back and speak to her. I'm so sorry. What did she say to you that you'd agree to that?"

I shook my head. "It was a threat. Don't worry about it." I

decided to deflect the conversation. "Why do some people call her Malavish? Do you know?"

"Malavish, from legend or myth, was being prepared by the goddesses Thielle and Nhor, among others, for her wedding. She was led astray from her intended—hence the name Malavish, whatever it was before. A broken promise, I think it means. Not in Obrone, but in some dialect to the north, I think. There was a great war about it."

"Oh! I think I remember hearing one version of the legend where she was kidnapped. Interesting that it echoes another great legend, like the weeping of spring," I said. "When Jammon betrayed Thielle for her ugly sister?"

"I guess. They call him Sethlans in other parts, did you know?"

"No, I think he's a different god," I said. "Sethlans is more of a blacksmith. Jammon is more of an artisan who made jewelry and worked with gold, silver, and gems." A crow laughed overhead and flew past, marking the trail before fading into the trees. "He was an alchemist, not someone who makes horseshoes or swords."

"Horseshoes are a new thing, after legend."

I laughed, glad to talk of much lighter things. I thought of old gods and what Grandmother Turani had said. Was that god Jammon or Sethlans, or both? An old god long gone, name forgotten like the counsel of gods that kept the Apatin at bay, or new gods—when does a new god become known? Maybe gods could transform with legends, like the shifting tales of Thielle or Sethlans.

"Too many stories told," he said. "The same could very well be said of Ravantha Malavish."

"Well, she is scary all the same. She may have wanted to

humiliate you, but I felt as if she wanted to... *possess* me."

We stopped for a while, catching our breath again.

"Yes, I'd wondered at that." He paused. "You look quite a lot like her, to my mind."

"You must be joking. She's beautiful." And she was.

Her hair was rich and thick, and long, though braided and styled for action. Her skin was tanned to a deep golden hue, and yet still seemed lighter than Cai's more olive skin tone or mine. She'd never be the sickly white like one of those northwest foreigners I'd seen on that one journey to the coast with Tages. She might have aged past traditional spinster age, but she was still lovely enough for men to desire. More, she was clearly physically strong without looking masculine or brutish. Only her attitude was ruthless and jarring from a woman that lovely.

I was either too cowed or too angered to remember I respected strong women. Velia was strong. But what is strength in a woman? It wasn't necessarily a woman who could ride and hunt like a man, because Velia could not. She ran a household and farm that earned her quite an income and lost none of her femininity in the process.

"Well, what's wrong with saying you're beautiful?" Cai said. "It's true. More, you could be right in that she may be more interested in you than me, for all that. I hope you make it back to Tages."

"I do, too."

We made haste through the rest of the land. We slept for a short time during the night and woke early. By the end of the next day, we crossed into Rasce's land. We built a thorn wall and slept without bothering to keep watch till rain woke us before dawn. We slogged through mud in the downpour. I dreaded mid-spring, knowing more mud and rain were to come. We only made it far enough into Rascenden to ensure that Cai was on the road back home.

"Are you sure you want to do that?" he asked. "Go back?"

"I'm sure I do not, but I made a promise. I must keep it. I have no intention of returning home late and earning the ire of Velia. Go, have a happy marriage, and do good work."

"I will," he said. "Thank you for walking with me!"

I turned and shouldered my promise to the lady of the land, as if shouldering added weight in my bag. I had, at least, some practice placating manipulative, strong women, and being Tages's apprentice was no small thing.

Chapter Six

—⟪◆⟫—

I waited on a bridge over a swollen river. It had been raining since I turned back, but I had some relief from the wet now. I leaned against a pillar to see the open, blue sky. I could not focus on my journal, even though it was the first time I'd had the opportunity to open it without risking it to the rain.

I thought of a broken branch and its still-frozen fall of leaves, and how the day's warmth let the poor tree weep into my hands.

I thought of Thielle weeping for spring.

I wondered about a woman called—by choice or not—Malavish, as if it was an epithet labeling her with blame for a marriage undone. How many tears did she weep? Who had she betrayed, or was *she* betrayed? Thinking about things I'd heard from listening to conversations with Velia and Tages, and Cai himself, I knew Ravantha had been the one betrayed.

I wasn't feeling a sense of empathy, though there was

certainly a good deal of sympathy for her based on what I knew. However, even with that, I had no desire to go further into Ravantha's land, except to leave it. I had promised to return so that she would not humiliate my friend.

I looked over my journal again, noting the places I wanted to stop and pick herbs after drawing them. I promised myself I would. I held onto it like a talisman for the future.

It was spring, time for things buried to come forth into new life. But there was a weeping that had to happen, in snowmelt, rain, or tears. Those tears fed buried bulbs, seeds, and roots of dormant trees, all buried against the cold of winter in a coverlet of leaves, growing in quiet, unseen power for their break from earth's womb and rise toward the sun.

All around me, on this journey, the early flowers of spring's promise were blooming or rising. I could still see some along the banks of the creek that was full of Thielle's tears.

How much weeping had there been for an abandoned baby? Did it matter if my natural mother had wept? Had Grandmother Turani not found me, I would have died with or without her weeping. I could still feel Grandmother Turani's arms around me and hear the echoes of her singing to me in Ndeb, and sometimes also in Obrone, so I could speak to those who came to her hut. She had not hidden that I was a foundling, but I'd never missed the love of mother or father. I had no sisters or brothers. I had not felt *any* lack! I hadn't even bothered to think of it till Thefare spoke to me at Hastia's healing.

I only discovered any sense of indifference after Grandmother Turani arranged my apprenticeship. Tages was content to bring me to his home as his apprentice. She had said she was going to the gods and needed to ensure that I would have an education. I did not know when she passed on, as Kuen-Tai hadn't come to tell me. I had no idea where she might have been buried, or if she even had been. She had always insisted that I not look for her.

"Be grateful for what I have taught you," Turani had said a few months before she'd gone, "that you can take of me; it will be with you always. Everything you find in my home is yours when you want it after I go to my sister, my twin."

A twin I'd never heard of till the past few years, and had no name for, or knew where she was—equally old, as well. My only family?

In this month of Thielle, twice now, a man and a woman claimed to know my past—as if *that* defined me better in their minds than all the work I had been doing with Tages, or the work I had been doing by myself or with Aule. Thinking of Ravantha, or Thefare, indifference was to be valued.

A broken branch in autumn wept from the water that betrayed the tree when it froze, and now the snowmelt tears turned dirt into mud, and swelled the stream with the sound of weeping. Would I be crying soon? I certainly felt as if something had broken inside me.

I heard a sound on the bridge, of footfalls on the wood. I looked up. To my amazement, it was a man, about Lady Ravantha's age. He was well dressed, quite calm and confident. There were no lines of worry around his eyes that I'd seen on Cai's face. His stride was easy, and his shoulders loose. I could see what Thefare's attempt at fashion was meant to be. The pants and coat looked good on him, and while clearly day clothes with the smell of horse on him, he looked far finer than the Lord of Thefarland could hope to be.

"The Lady would like to see you," he said.

I was wary. Ravantha had set no time or place to meet. I shuddered at the thought that she'd known when I entered her lands again.

"Who are you?" I asked, surprised he was her envoy. He was, for one, a man, and handsome. He was broad-shouldered, tall, and athletic. His hair was deep brown, which the sun had given reddish tints. His profile could have been on coins.

"Larce. I'm a friend of Marce, who would have wed Ravantha. We come to visit when we can."

I decided to be bold and bite back against my discomfort. "My friend Cai, who Ravantha insulted, mentioned there might be some kind of ill will about the wedding. You come openly?"

"Of course. My Lord Aranthur, Marce's father, has no problems with us visiting another noble person in her own land, even if it irritates her father, Lord Rasce. Aranthur still has hopes of some advantage."

"I understood she disliked men on her lands," I said, having had excellent evidence of that already, considering her threat to Cai.

Larce shook his head. "That's a bit of an exaggeration of the truth. She does not *trust* men with single women, or men traveling alone who might visit villages on their path, and with reason."

And yet she trusted this man to guide me, a single woman, through her lands.

"I noticed that there were no villages on the road we took," I said.

"They are off the through paths, but all villages are still connected through the land. She prefers people to travel *through* the Westvell, and not linger, especially men, unless for trade."

"So, she threatens them if they linger too long?"

"Not generally," he said with amusement. "But they are often escorted out by fathers and brothers at need. If she's demanded that all young women on her lands learn to defend themselves, there's a reason for her law. Come."

I put on my shoulder bag, using both straps. I wanted both arms free near this man. However good a steward of her land—and this was interesting—she'd been cruel and sharp when I'd met her. Ravantha's behavior toward Cai now made me even more nervous. I wondered if she'd threatened him only to force me to promise I'd see her. This was no good augury of a lasting friendship.

"Do you know what she wants to speak to me about?"

"No, but I have my guesses, now that I see you."

"And they are?"

"My own to keep for now."

We walked a while, passing a small village with a wall against predators surrounding the cluster of huts. We walked through more woods, which suddenly opened up to cultivated fields. Some that had already been planted with early crops, and others where people were preparing for later spring planting.

Above the fields was a large manor house up on a mountain rock outcropping. It was clearly newer than the ruins Cai and I had found, with the three chimneys and strange Tree, or even Grandmother Turani's house, but I could see the echoes of that rustic, bold style. Whoever updated this building should have worked for Thefare. This blend of old and new worked. The house reflected the landscape around it and, while surprising to me with its mostly unfamiliar modern style, it was beautiful.

Ravantha Malavish stood on a ledge high above us, with a spear in her hand. As much as I did not want to be here or visit with her, I thought the scene and her, in that moment, quite impressive.

Another man met us at the bottom of the hill. I was surprised at Larce's shift. As soon as he caught sight of the man, his body seemed ready to leap, like a hunter at prey. He looked his friend over anxiously.

They could have been brothers, though this man's brown hair was so sun-kissed it seemed burnished with gold and curlier. He was a bit smaller than Larce, but by my guide's deference, this man was clearly the dominant or richer man.

"Marce!" Larce cried out.

Aranthur's son. Marce and Larce? I tried not to gawp at their names.

"You found her then, Larce," he said. "I was sure you'd get lost."

"I did indeed, Marce. But I know my way. If you'd gone, we'd have been searching for you already!" he teased back. Larce took Marce's bags, as if he were a servant. I could recognize the look of a person checking over a patient. I thought back to Velia and Tages's discussion about Aranthur. Despite the fact that the two men grinned at each other, and clearly knew each other well, I was on guard and looked at Marce with a Doctor-Diviner's eye.

"Ready to leave?" Larce asked.

"Where are you going?" I asked.

"Her rules, till she can wed: No man lives in her home. We stay in the village we passed. Go on. The path is clearly marked."

I watched them leave, keeping an eye on not the protective Larce, but for whatever sign he had been looking for. There was a slight tremble in Marce's hand, but nothing more till a sudden jerking movement, which had Larce quickly steady him. I stored the information for later research—till I could get to Tages's library —and turned to the waiting lady.

I went up the lonely path. The steps were carved out of stone. Age had smoothed some of the chipping away, but I could see, here and there, where the old carving marks still blazed out as if the stone had suffered in the pounding of tools. She stood at the top, spear in hand, waiting for me.

"Come, Sen of the Woods. It will be dark soon, and we do not have a wall to guard us, only this high rock."

I followed her in, feeling as if I'd willingly entered some trap. I noticed that she used the spear like a cane, as if unsteady on her feet. She sat quickly and gestured for me to join her.

"Are you all right?" I asked, unable to stop my professional inquiry.

"Yes, of course," she said, but her lips were pursed with indignation at my question.

There was food laid out for us on a sturdy, but beautifully made table in her main hall. A few servant women filled our goblets and then disappeared to their tasks or rooms. I waited for her to eat first and drink first. She was far more noble than I, and I needed to show as much respect as I could, no matter my distrust. I was glad for all of Velia's instruction on etiquette.

"You do not speak," she said.

"I have nothing to say."

"You are not curious as to who your parents might be?"

"No. Not at all. What need do I have for people who did not want me?"

She paused from putting a forkful of food in her mouth,

carefully laying it back down on her plate. "You think they did not want you?"

I shrugged. "Grandmother Turani found me exposed in the woods—alone, of course, and with someone's real expectation of my dying. Babies cannot survive without milk. Even adults, depending on the season, can suffer without shelter from the elements, if predators don't kill them first. What else am I to think?"

"You have a point. Let me tell you a brief tale." Ravantha took a bite of food, chewed, and swallowed it with some wine while carefully considering her words. She put fork and wine down and focused all her attention on me. Her eyes bored into me like an awl. I gritted my teeth against the pain of it.

"There was a woman who was to be married," she said. "Her father was negotiating part of her inheritance and dowry— what she would take with her when she wed. But she was raped, and with child before they could have her officially betrothed. She gave birth. Her father, who was furious that she'd had a girl—a baby *girl* who ruined his hopes for an alliance—took that child away. He exposed her to die. And yet here she is."

I gaped at her. The warmth of one spring morning made a broken branch *drip, drip, drip* into my open hands. This was freezing, breaking, and weeping all in one.

It wasn't what I expected.

My armpits dripped. My back pricked with sweat. I forced my breath to be steady, in an effort to keep any tone of ridicule out of my words, in exercising the compassion my role demanded.

"You think I'm your daughter."

A strange surge of hope filled me. A dizzying vision of a different life made me nearly faint. She could be my mother, and I would have family and a home. But I was repelled by that same thought. The only thought I'd had for my mother (or father) was deep resentment—with or without a sense of loss. That resentment flared up and burnt the hope.

She was a strong woman, I knew. Her land was prosperous and well-run, from what I had seen. She might be a mother to be proud of. And yet, I did not think a mother should look upon a daughter with quite so much possession, as if I were a thing, something symbolic like a broken necklace made by a god.

My resentment burnt out, staring at the eyes filled with so much longing, replaced by a deep sense of discomfort. It was as if my bones and my skin made way to becoming filled by what she wanted, not who I was. It was just as dizzy-making as the one I'd had myself.

With some strange flash of remembrance turned into an apt analogy: Thielle's temple of love and harmony becoming a den of prostitution. I doubt she wanted to prostitute me, but she wanted something from me, wanted me to be someone I knew I was not.

Ravantha sighed, with something between wistfulness and peace. "You have my coloring and look so much like me and my sister that I cannot but think so."

"Women give birth all the time. And many people of this region look alike. There are many girls my age." Hastia was one of them, for instance. I knew there must be other girls in not just Rascenden or Thefarland, but also the Westvell, of similar age.

"No. Actually not. My midwife was clear that there were no women who were pregnant at the same time in our area or beyond. Not in the same stage."

I said nothing to this.

Statistically, it really didn't matter. For one, she could have no idea of my age. No one did, actually. Grandmother Turani had never said. I could only assume somewhere around sixteen to eighteen years. It might be less, or more, but it was a reasonable guess. Velia and Tages believed eighteen, mainly because of Tages's visits to Turani.

It was also not the time to bring out various studies of obstetrics that went beyond the plain language of midwifery. She was clearly not a midwife, and she did not need to be Velia to understand that babies born early often died. In all her years of experience, Velia had helped only one child survive an early birth. That child survived, in my opinion, because of her deep stubbornness, and breathing—very, very gently—into its young, weak lungs. The child was, unfortunately, sickly and prone to any lung infection in the area.

It was unlikely I was an early child. I was too healthy, in general. Ravantha's daughter might have been, too. I did not know. No one could.

She continued. "When you were born was important, and when another woman had given birth in the same timespan was vital because of my needing a wet nurse for you."

I shook my head. A wet nurse did not have to have babies at the same time. Her child could be weaned early or share the breast with a younger baby.

"If I could pretend I had not given birth," said Ravantha, "my father wanted me to wed as soon as possible, but the moment I held you in my arms, I fell so deeply in love I could not part with you. My father could not bear that, and when I rested from my birthing labors, he took you from my arms. He might have merely been content to keep you, had you been a boy. It did not matter.

He discovered that Marce's father, Lord Aranthur, refused to consider the marriage when he learned I could not bring the dower my father had promised him."

"What was that?"

"Not this house or these lands, prosperous as it is. Aranthur wanted Jammon's necklace—Jammon's or Thielle's, depending on which legend you read or hear. Part of Thielle's wedding necklace is in Thefare's treasure house. My father had tried to negotiate an exchange of *that* necklace for *these* lands before I was raped. Lord Aranthur wanted that as part of his wealth, not this land, locked far away from his influence. Thefare refused to give it to us after his brother Fuluns's assault."

"Why not?" I asked, thinking of Ati's gold necklace.

"As much as he was ready to murder him, Thefare did not want to admit his brother forced me. Doing so, he'd lose not just the land he had attempted to negotiate for, but also that necklace. Fuluns said I tempted him, and went off alone with him, in my fancy city clothes."

I shook my head, thinking of Ati and her uplifted breasts that caressed a gold imitation. I also thought of Arntlei's missing husband and Hastia's father.

"I don't know why you care to tell me this when it could not possibly matter to me."

She shook her head, rejecting my words. "I had given up all hope you were alive."

I had never been a secret, though few higher-born people had ever visited Grandmother Turani. There was no reason for people not to know I existed. Thefare knew me as Turani's adopted child, even to my name. As calmly as I could, I deflected that statement. "Regardless of who my parents are, I am bound to the Doctor-Diviner Tages as his apprentice."

"I understand. But there is so much I want to teach you," she said and resumed her meal, her air confident, as if she could offer me something beyond my apprenticeship.

"Being taught by Tages is not enough?" I asked incredulously. "Tages is renowned in the area, even beyond Lord Rasce's land, which is your father's lands. Even Aranthur beyond has asked for his aid."

I could not help but shake my head in bafflement. This was stranger than her claim that I was her daughter. Tages's reputation in these lands alone ought to have been sufficient accolades to his skill in teaching. I happened to know there was far, far more. There were great scholars of science, such as Vesalus, who transformed the study of anatomy—because he actually was brave enough to look into a human body once it had deceased, without fear of ancestors being infuriated—as well as a leader in botany and biology, such as Numesen or my friend Cuintus up in Jambrone. Tages was beginning to cultivate scholars within the growing science of chemistry that had danced its way away from the metaphysics of alchemy. All the while, there were Doctor-Diviners around the country who wrote to him for advice on the more mystical side of our work. Aule had told me that Tages was the only reason there were men who believed our healing art had not been complete quackery.

"I sent spies to inquire after you after we met. Easy to do, as he often sends me herbs for the headaches I've had since my attack."

Headache and probable dizziness? I thought this was interesting. But I said nothing.

"He keeps you at a lesser level."

Apprentice

I haven't been with him even half a year, I wanted to say, but she spoke before I could protest.

"And his training is not nearly enough!" she said, slapping her hand on the table. "He will not teach a girl how to defend herself," she said. Her tones were emphatic. "Think: You are beautiful. Men will desire you and demand to have what they want—especially realizing that you have no family to protect you. I did have family to protect me—for nothing!"

Again, I was bewildered. Few people in this region would importune me for any reason. I had the office of being an active and respected apprentice Doctor-Diviner in my own right, as well as being the apprentice of my mentor.

"I am not your subject. I am not bound by your law."

"It is not enough. You will need more than that once it becomes clear you are my daughter."

I shook my head again. "How in the world could that matter? There is no way you could prove it."

"Thefare hasn't seen you yet, or he would make use of you."

Thefare had, in fact, seen me recently. And he had made some indication that he knew who my parents were. I shivered against the damp of my sweat. I wondered if her wish for me to know how to defend myself might be necessary. I had no desire to bind myself to her, or Thefare for that matter, regardless of the provocation. She herself ought to understand it. Her father, Marce's father, and even Thefare had treated her like a game piece. She did not realize she was doing the same to me.

"There are only two things I want in the world," she said.

"And those are?"

"To know my daughter and to get Thielle's necklace from

Thefare. I know Aranthur wants it for healing, for reparations of the fouled marriage—that he'd get paid for the ruined negotiations, not me. If it's anyone's, it's *mine*, paid for with my blood spilled on his treasure room floor, and from the humiliation and broken promises by *all* of them."

"And yet you let Marce come and visit you."

"He and Larce teach me how to use weapons. He understands that if I'd known how to defend myself, Fuluns would have been bleeding and unconscious on that floor, not *me*."

I paused. I had not eaten anything. If I had been hungry, the conversation changed that. I had not had any of her wine. "Can I go now? You've told me all you wanted to tell me. I need to get back on the road."

"You cannot go out at night. You would get caught by wild animals."

I did not say that I felt as if I'd been captured by a great beast already. She may not have wanted to roast me over a fire and lay me out on a platter for her dining pleasure, but I felt like she was a predator, and I was prey.

Even her idea of teaching me self-defense seemed thin. It was a means to hold me in her grasp. Granted, I thought she had every right to learn how to defend herself. She saw a looming threat over me, where I saw none—excepting her.

"May I then rest? I have far to go in the morning," I asked.

"Yes, of course," she said.

She gave me a chamber of my own, for which I was grateful. I yearned for my hard pallet in Tages's workroom, or even some gathered leaves in the cover of Grandmother Turani's old house.

I woke during the night. I heard my door open. I did not

move and pretended sleep. There was only a soft noise of someone sitting in the chair nearby. I was not comfortable knowing that Ravantha must be watching me. Cai's teasing advances never felt this menacing. I certainly teased him just as much about dissection, but had never forced him, for instance, to eat any raw intestines, or some animal's heart or liver, or ever turned intestines into a belt for him. He would say no and I'd stop teasing him—even if I'd try yet again to help him understand what a liver looked like.

In teasing each other about things neither of us would do, we were equal. We never crossed boundaries. We both could laugh. That's not to say that he would not have gladly taken my maidenhead if I'd been willing, but he cheerfully let go of hope when it was clear that I was not interested. He never blamed me for a no. We'd been alone many, many times, deep in the woods, and he'd never pushed matters.

Ravantha's watching over me while I slept proved she had no respect for my boundaries.

As soon as I sensed she had fallen asleep during her vigil, I quietly gathered up my things and left. I let moon and starlight guide me. Making good time, I was halfway to her borders by dawn. I plunged ahead till I made the ruins, where I climbed to the top and slept under the Tree that Cai could not see. I fell asleep and dreamed.

Chapter Seven

―――――《‹•›》―――――

I woke screaming from a tangle of bodies. It had been no mere dream. It was not a nightmare, though it felt like one. In the dream, Ravantha had been listening to an argument, and I was reminded of when I had done the same earlier in the month. She, with her ear to a closed door, and I, from one open door, and then in a tree. Aranthur was, again, a feature in the argument.

I recognized Thefare's voice. He shouted, "You are just his agent. I will give Aranthur nothing! And not this necklace to add to his collection of godly relics! He's insulted me too much!"

The other man's tones were emphatic. "Whatever he's done to you, I'm making a better offer than he ever made you! For a broken bit of necklace. Just give me that piece of jewelry no one can wear anyway, and you will have the property you know you want and need!"

"Compared to all his wealth, this necklace is proof of my lineage, my honor, my pride!"

I thought, even during the dream, and again upon waking: *It came to you by women.* I didn't need the fading matrilineal customs of the lands to tell me that with the historic crisis of dying cattle, men's wealth was no longer nomadic or movable. Men had to own property, like women. I gave a wry laugh. *For some men, that must have been a blow to their ego.* But I'd known it, because somehow, I'd been in the heart of the necklace, inside that amber gem's golden glow. It was powerful. It was something the completed copy would never be, however gilded.

While I'd heard the argument quite well from two men unseen behind closed doors, I didn't have to guess at the other players.

Featured in the vision was Ravantha, Fuluns, and the precious, ancient, and broken necklace of a goddess. He'd hung it around her neck. His hands filled in for the missing chain—creating an embrace, and a trap. In the final moments of Ravantha's rape, the tarnished silver and beads and gems had clattered to the floor, loud as if those things made thunder. It had woken me.

My head throbbed, and I did not know if it was from that fall or an echo of sympathy for Ravantha.

Not wanting to revisit the horrific vision of what happened to her, I thought of the goddess's bauble. I could see it clearly, almost as if I'd been looking at it through a mirror.

The necklace had been clearly damaged over the ages and could never be worn unless fixed, assuming the missing parts were found. It had broken off just above the left side of the main gem, an amber held in a leaf shape curled around it, and another leaf above. There was one dangling pendant, a small piece of amber, mingled in with a few amber stones. Whatever the original pattern or design, this was a mess of broken links. The chain was dark with age, and though some of the edges of the pendant's leaf shape were also dark, the silver gleamed with the light. To me, it seemed to gleam with the amber's inner light.

The memory of that inner light brought me back into the vision.

"No!" I yelled, standing up, leaning against the trunk of the Tree.

I don't know why I had seen this vision of the past. I huddled under the branches, gasping for breath. Within an amber glow, I could see again Fuluns tricking Ravantha into being alone with him. He'd offered to show her what her father was asking for in exchange for her entire, extensive property.

A tarnished, broken necklace, asked for in exchange for all her wealthy property?

As much as I valued all that made Medicine work, from ancestors to the other side of nature that was unseen, the Divinity in all things, even that necklace was not at all worth what had been done to her. Aranthur was a madman to desire it. How could a damaged necklace heal? Especially one less valued than the replica made in gold?

The last image stuck in my mind was of Ravantha's hand doing more damage to the necklace and grasping onto a couple of amber beads and one small pendant. Thankfully, I did not dream more, but I knew that they'd found her there, where Fuluns had left her, having beaten her head to the ground till she'd passed out as he had his way with her.

Shock and disgust shifted to anger. No wonder Thefare had banished Fuluns. He could have had lands that were—from what I had seen—of fair income. And yet why hesitate in the negotiations? His pride? The necklace was useless to him. Getting the Westvell should have been an easy choice. I did not know how close he had come to accepting. It was probably an easy negotiation on his part, no matter how much he'd protested and haggled.

It would have been the most logical choice.

I thought Thefare must value his brother greatly. Fuluns deserved far more punishment than banishment for what he'd done to Ravantha. He certainly couldn't claim it was consensual, what with all the blood on the floor, and with her being unconscious from a head wound.

I would have laid bets that Tages had helped her survive.

The nightmare, and its implications—as well as a deep knowledge that the dream was real—left me raw and nauseated. I could not help but weep. The girl who had entered that treasure room to look at the necklace was far and away not the same woman I'd met. My stomach churned, and I threw up bile.

I felt bruised, having slept on the rocks. I hugged the Tree and looked up at small buds above me, almost pink. As I cried, some of the buds opened up at the first blush of dawn, and some of the petals fell upon my head. The petals were like white tears of the Tree, crying in sympathy.

When I felt calmer, I stood up. There were awful thoughts in my head. One was wondering how Ati felt putting on her jewelry for great celebrations, having to step over stains of Ravantha's blood. I shuddered again. It would be now, for me, a powerful symbol of what women had given up to men.

I knew the dream was real. I had some idea of when a vision was fashioned by desires of my mind and when it was not.

This was not my own fabrication.

I realized that Ravantha's rape hadn't been about sex, but power over a woman who had, Fuluns felt, dismissed him. He'd wanted her. Her father had refused. He'd married another. And in one act, he defiled her, her father, his brother, and the gods. If *ancestors* could make a person ill from disapproval or a sense of neglect, what would gods do? I had a sense that exiling Fuluns was in hopes of regaining regard. The brother had offended the gods, perhaps, and so luck, fate, and finances crumpled under the weight of such defilement. Ancestors would have made the man sick; the gods made the land poor.

The rage Thefare might have felt—should have felt—was, I knew, my own imagining.

However powerful a symbol it might be, an awful threshold to step across from when women owned the houses and property and men moved cattle in nomadic patterns, to where men claimed a great deal of all property and defined society.

There was one woman who had defied that set of rules. However much harm had come to her, Ravantha ruled her own lands. I remembered there were other women who did not let men define them. I thought of Velia. She owned her own house in the compound, and she also owned cattle. However much she bound herself to Tages, those things remained true. I thought of the Doctor-Diviner Zelia, who was also respected for her craft. It was not her fault that science was growing, and our craft was dying in the hands of fools.

I took some of the fallen blossoms into my hands, let others weep down into them, petals falling off the tree. With the same certainty, I also could see that one of the reasons Thefare had hesitated in a negotiation that ought to have been so easy was pride. Each time Aranthur, or any of those he sent, attempted to barter for the bauble, it meant someone richer, more powerful, had come begging. Had come begging to *him*, to Thefare, and all his need for unreasonable respect.

Poor Aranthur, defied so many times over. Tages refused to give him healing, considering him a fool. Thefare refused him out of piqued pride. The memory of the discussion between Tages and Velia came back to me, and I thought: *Is he* still *trying to get that thing?* The necklace's power was legend, and yet... I knew that it had never given to anyone what it had brought me. Its powers lost to men.

I tried to let go of the amber-gold colored vision, but could not. It lingered like the stink of nightmare sweat.

I stretched and then shook my body, but it felt as if my whole body was held in amber sap, dripping from the dying side of the tree. Crow cackled at me from the branches above. I did not look. I did not want to see—but I knew it all the same—that Crow had an amber bead in its beak.

"Go back to Nhor," I said, "And her Ugly Grotto... or the school of anatomy. Whichever you prefer!" I cried out to her.

The spirit of all crows merely laughed at me, and that without dropping the bead.

I gathered up my things and did the only thing I knew to do, and that was to work. I made my way home, stopping to collect plants, samples of plants for my press, and to take notes or draw various forms of nature, including drawings of animals in various stages of disrepair. Some of those drawings were important, because damage might help me understand what predator had taken the animal, which would in turn help if a human victim was unable to speak to me and say what had hurt them—assuming they lived long enough for either Tages or me to save them. Life and death were held in balance by our hands.

My shoulder bag was full of plants for our garden, and I also tracked at least one pride of lions and a pack of jackals near some villages.

I crossed one lone trail of a jackal, which was an unusual sight. They rarely went rogue. Tages could inform the village chiefs, though I alerted one hunter I passed on my second day about the rogue jackal. He was herding a small group of cattle for market and was glad of the warning. But he also grinned.

"Jackal is crafty," he said. "Odd that he'd leave tracks for you to see, but you're a student of Tages?"

I nodded.

"We'll keep a watch out for his friends."

I walked till I was exhausted, slept little, and kept moving. Even while often stopping to do my proper work, I believed I had made excellent time.

Tages looked up at me as I opened the door to the study side of his round house. "You have flowers in your hair," he said.

"Oh?" I reached up and took a still-fresh flower from my head. It had been three days. I held the flower in my hand, looking at its simple pink and white beauty.

"Did you draw this plant?" he asked.

"No," I said, regretfully. I had wanted to escape the vision. I said, "It was from a Tree. But I did draw others."

He took a blossom from my hair. "I have not seen a flower quite like this. I would like a picture of this Tree. Can you find it again?"

"Yes, and gladly," I said. Despite the dream, I wanted to go back there again. I wanted to know more about this Tree, and try to remember the lullaby. "There's a horse tied to the tree out front," I said. "Is Aule home?"

Velia came into the room. "We have a guest," she said, in a cheerful frame of mind. "Please freshen up and make sure Cai's hut is ready for her." She walked past in one of her more elaborate robes and out the door, presumably to the bathing hut.

"Her?" I asked Tages.

"Yes, the Lady Ravantha is here to speak with me," said Tages. "She's in the bathing hut after her travels."

So, I did not return to a long-expected visit from Aule, but to someone I had no wish to see.

"I'll go make sure her hut is ready, then." I pulled out my journal and press, and put my bag down. "Here are my field notes. I think there's a new hunting ground for a mountain lion a day away—east of Grandmother Turani's home," I said. "A bit close to Thielfar village and their cattle."

"I'll let Thefare and the hunters know."

I left without any other show of temper. I was infuriated that Ravantha was here. I knew what she wanted. Me. I did not want to be her daughter, and I still felt bruised by the rocks I'd slept on, dreaming of her rape. It was too close, too invasive a knowledge of her. My bruises had already faded. Her bruises and scars from that night, however, were obviously still unhealed. They went further deep than her flesh, down into her veins and bones, and had every right to be.

Mab Morris

I did not want her to be my mother.

The crowning of blossoms fell from my head as I went out the door, a trail of petals weeping. As I made my way to the hut, the rain began to fall.

Chapter Eight

———————— ⟪◆⟫ ————————

The month of the Apatin, mid-spring

My shoulders sagged, looking at the hut. I felt as flat as my hair would get from the rain if I stood out there much longer. Dread for the work of the season took the sting out of my temper. There wasn't much to do *now*, but there soon would be.

Mid-spring was the time of rain, when Thielle's tears were joined by the rain from the God of Weather. The Apatin, or Father Rain, was always with "the," never just Apatin. Legends and history never said why. I had my own guesses. There was more to him than just one aspect. For instance, the Apatin had three kinds of lightning bolts in his hands: those of warning, intervention, and direct catastrophe. He could not, a Father God though he was, use the latter two without permission from the consultant or hidden gods—whoever *they* were. Their legends were even older, and their history even longer lost.

I wondered, at times, what those hidden gods thought as their stories faded, the way the lore of the Doctor-Diviners was fading even now in the face of science. Did they fade in helpless regret? Were they old enough to go senile like Grandmother Turani, who had been old when she'd found me? Or did they, like I was trying to do, write their lore into the words of the new sciences?

Did they reinvent themselves? Or had they been reinvented?

As long as it rained soft and steady, and not every single day, the month of Apatin was good for the future harvest. By legend, the Apatin had been infuriated by Jammon's—or Sethlans's, depending on the region of Obrone where the stories were told—choosing of the ugly twin, Nhor, instead of Thielle. Whatever early flowers had not yet broken through the prisoning ground of winter with Thielle's tears were now fed by these rains. I longed for those spring blossoms, which signaled the end of rain.

With storms, Velia would frantically paint rafters with spells and pleas against Tigna, Father Rain's evil alter ego. When the Apatin defied the counsel or hidden gods, he became Tigna, the evil spirit that caused damaging lightning strikes, adding hail to his arsenal. Tigna also caused mildew, which was a disaster that sometimes lingered far longer than storm damage, ruining clothes, food, seeds, and grain, and often caused illness. I would have to clean everything and the spells when the storm was through. Every time. And in all the damp, attempting to battle mold and mildew in the meantime.

Soft rain, or heavy, it was a month of mud. Cleaning either building would involve quite a lot of it. For now, it was not a difficult job. I was reluctant all the same. I got the one-room hut ready for our guest, not caring that Ravantha would have a muddy journey back to her home. She would take the mud with her.

I went back into the main house at a dash, and only got a little bit muddy at the feet, and was glad that I had fresh clothes at my pallet.

I noted the two women talking. Ravantha clearly was ill from a ride that had been, no doubt, too fast for her head. In the other room, Tages was working on a brew to help her.

"How do you control your property?" Velia was asking Ravantha, as she prepared a light meal, one clearly not taxing to one's stomach, already accompanied by severe headache pain. An unusual midday treat in a land with only a morning and evening meal.

"I was damaged in the eyes of my father and needed to be put away. I made use of it. I made a choice."

"So, you saw a problem, and..."

"Made changes, made choices."

I spoke up. "You remain friends with your former betrothed. Could he not have married you? Chosen you?"

"Marriage with me? After a time, I was glad I rejected any renewed offers. It would have removed me from my one place of power, the one place where I could make my own choices. I legitimately own the land. While I must honor his overrule, I could demand my father never visit. I removed him from influence. I also removed Marce and his father's influence by refusing marriage when I was more sound of mind."

"Do you consider marriage to remove a woman's power? I lost nothing marrying Tages," Velia offered.

"Not all, but I see it often enough, even in my own land. If a woman is unable to make choices for her own good, or the good of the family, then yes. A woman must be able to change the circumstances that negatively impact the good of the household. If she cannot, then the marriage is not good." With a shrewd look at Velia, she added, "Times have changed. Women used to have more power. Now? You see it. For many, what else is she but chattel, and only as good as the cows or house she brought to the union?"

I stared at her, realizing that Ravantha, however damaged her brain might be, was and could be quite intelligent and reasoning. However irrational her tempers, I would not discount her. I agreed, in principle, to Ravantha's statement. I certainly understood her need for power and security. I, too, would never want to be chattel.

Tages came in just then, and the scene shifted.

"You ride your horse too hard," he said to his guest. "It is not good for your head."

She said, "But I had to come. I am sure you have proof she is my daughter."

He gave Ravantha a tincture to drink.

"We do not," said Velia, "but we will, one way or another."

"How?" I asked.

"Well, who her ancestors are will tell us. Soon we will do a ritual, an adept test. What else to do in this rain?"

"And can I be there for that?" asked Ravantha.

Both Velia and Tages shook their head.

"I will say that Grandmother Turani said my parents were not in this world," I said, sharing a glittering, but brief memory.

"Even *I* heard she was senile," Ravantha said. "So, I will hope."

"It was a long way to come when we could give you no proof," Tages said.

"I had to ask," she said.

"If she's yours, she will see your ancestors in the ritual," said Velia. "Can you trust that I will let you know?"

Ravantha nodded and had to make peace with that.

"Now, you must rest after your ride."

I was sent to take Ravantha's bags to the hut. I was wet through by the time I was done.

She did not stay long, and I was glad.

After she left, the next few days we prepared for my initiation test. She came a week later, staying on a few nights. She did not make many demands on my time, which did nothing to lessen my distrust of her.

The rides were difficult for Ravantha. We tended her for at least a day. The minute she arrived, Tages prepared brews that would help with her dizziness and headaches, although the symptoms did not always appear immediately.

On that second visit, Tages had me help him brew some infusions while Velia tended her in the bath. "There's balm in here," I said to him. "You are not just taking care of headache or dizziness, are you?"

"Of course. Now tell me what you know of long-term head injuries—the kind that do not bleed." Another quizzing. He and Velia had been testing my knowledge for days.

I thought of my vision and dreams. Fuluns had rendered her unconscious, banging her head against the floor to silence her cries. "You are suggesting something beyond concussion," I said. "Which might have symptoms for a few days..."

"Or, depending on the severity, years," he prompted.

"This was more than that, I think. The brain jostled onto both sides of the skull, so..." I thought for a moment. "Headache, dizziness, and... irrational outbursts of anger."

"Yes. Tell me more. You've read Vesalus and others."

"We don't know where in the brain such injuries occur—or if it matters," I said. "I know you have the theory that it matters *where* the injury occurs, but it's not proven yet. It's easy to imagine a smaller, softer object would still bang against the harder container, adding to its injury."

"We do not have the ability to see the unseen," Tages said.

"What an awful thing to hear from a Doctor-*Diviner*!" I teased. "But we do know more than your mentor did."

"*You* know more than my mentor did, even before you came to me as an apprentice!" he said with a snort. "Our colleagues might as well be the witch doctors the city folk call them, going to their physicians and dying because they still did not get the aid they needed."

"Her head injuries were severe," I said. "Will she suffer from it all her life?"

"Her headaches were becoming less frequent, till recently, due to, I suspect, the jostling riding a horse seemed to give her head. I gathered she'd been walking more than riding in the past. I'd not had need to send her as much medication till lately."

"She's still irrational," I said, with betraying venom. "Causing herself the harm easily remedied by not riding."

"You merely do not trust her," he said, pointedly.

"Very true." I paused. "We still have some oat straw in the cupboard."

"Her outbursts are not hysterical in the same sense, Sen."

"Yes, sir," I said. "I am not considering it the misused term found in books Aule has sent home..."

"It originated with a term for the womb in a different culture," he pointed out.

"Yes, but I will state that I do not see it as the *supposed* irrational female over-excitement, or feminine overdramatic behavior." I paused in thought. Women were often viewed as such, but in the very few mysteries of femininity Velia did share with me, it was more often caused by limitations placed upon them by men.

She had said, *"A helpless explosion coming forth, retaining a sense of self-identity and power after suppression, and just as firmly put down by the ridicule of terms like hysteria, as if those emotions have just as little legitimacy as they've had voice."* The memory gave me pause. I clearly had to think. My dislike of Ravantha was clouding my view. "It is irrational behavior caused by injury, *not* because she was born with a womb."

"List me the varying causes of these irrational emotions," he demanded. "In a paper after we finish."

I did so, not obfuscating those often displayed by women, but added to what could be considered a Doctor-Diviner lexicon. I realized that it was information I could add to my notes. I was building a book of not merely plants, but a lexicon of ailments. I added those irrational behaviors that were certainly displayed by men in very different ways. I did not neglect to elaborate on how they compared to those inspired by head injuries. It was an interesting test; it was also a lesson. It taught me a great deal. In my growing reference book, I added the herbs that our lore suggested to aid such things, but also those found in books Aule had sent from the university.

It was a short paper, similar to Aule's university work. Writing that paper, I realized I could spend years on this study: a comparative study of the mystical work I was learning with Tages and the new sciences.

I did not speak more, after that, and merely brewed her tea upon request, adding perhaps more of the balm than he'd requested. The needs of the paper had given me time to pause. I stepped back and observed Ravantha with less defensiveness.

It was clear that she intended to return, but a day before she left, when she implied this intent, Tages informed her that it would not be possible for her to lodge in the compound for the remainder of the month, as his son, Aule, would be returning home for a stay. "If you wish to return, despite the difficulty of the journey for your head, you might find welcome in the manor?" he said, probably knowing this was not possible for her. I wondered how much he'd been irritated by her visits.

It was an indirect yet pointed statement of *Please stay home.*

His statement elicited a response from Velia. "Aule is coming home?" Her face was bright with pleasure.

Tages waved the letter.

"Yes, and he's bringing equipment—if it survives the journey in all this mud and rough travel."

"Equipment?" she asked, before I could.

"Yes," he said and turned back to his patient and guest. "This equipment will help me make extracts stronger than these infusions. They will help you get better, I think, and be more easily transported to your home."

Ravantha could only accept. I could see that he had maneuvered her into not riding the distance for her health, yet I was delighted.

Tages had waved Ravantha off. It would be some time before Aule returned. He wanted me to undergo that mystical test.

Chapter Nine

—— «‹•›» ——

V elia helped me prepare for the initiatory adept test. She gave me fresh clothes, but also some teas to purge my system.

"This is important," she said. "With Cai gone, Tages needs another adept to train and learn the spirit side of the work."

Bathed and drinking tea, she led me in meditation as my body purged. Empty body, empty mind.

To my surprise, there really wasn't much ritual to the ritual, unless it was in part the cleaning of the body and spending the day in preparation. It was certainly not as elaborate as a Milk Tree ceremony that took three days. Then we called upon our ancestors, and Tages gave me a piece of mushroom to eat. It tasted like dung and earth.

I realized very quickly that this mushroom was part of all three rivers Grandmother Turani used to talk about. One was of the earth, but also the living. Like other mushrooms, it asked the trees about the sunlight and told the trees about the earth below.

However, this one also spoke about cows. A particular cow, the rivers and the land it walked, how it chewed its cud, was sometimes painlessly bled to feed hunters, and felt safe in a wattle fence as lions roared in the moonlight.

"Now it is important for you to tell me about the ancestors you see," Tages was saying as I was learning about and experiencing the nature of this mushroom.

"Remember all you can for later," said Velia, "if you wander." She was looking pensive.

"You will notice that it will wake your senses, and you will feel or see things you would not have before," Tages said. "It will probably feel unusual to you."

"I hope this works," Velia muttered as she turned away to drink her own tea and nibble on a piece of mushroom as well.

There was nothing really unusual, as yet. I wandered around memories while sitting and waiting, letting Tages and Velia sit across from me, staring, waiting for any sign that I saw or noticed anything different.

I remembered Grandmother Turani telling me a story about Thielle, Nhor, and Jammon, and the necklace he'd made. She'd cackled about it, how they'd gotten it wrong. "That's what time does, and it was so long ago."

I'd already come to understand the great difficulty of senility, where stories rambled, moved around a timeline, and could be both coherent and strange. I could see that great Tree rising over me, gleaming in the sunlight and starlight, even while I could hear ants climbing up the dead side, eating at it. I heard the lullaby's hummed tune, as if coming from the wind in the leaves.

I did see, as I had felt before, the guides or ancestors of Tages and Velia. I felt the same distinct, but hazy presence, as in everyday life, but I could see them better, hear them better. The women were round and robust, the men sturdy on Velia's family side. Tages's family, they were all lean, the men with vibrant but stringy musculature. The guides beside Tages were silent. They sat waiting, watching.

I looked for myself, but there were no people.

I only noticed the Tree and the shining divinity on either side of it. The branches embraced the goddesses on either side, even as their arms curled around the trunk.

Velia was getting agitated. "Still no one?" she asked. "Nothing unusual?"

"I don't see anything unusual," I admitted. "The details are clear, but it's what I notice every day. I'm certainly not seeing or sensing anyone who would claim me, or whom I could claim as an ancestor. I am seeing the Tree I told Tages about, but it's probably just an exaggerated memory."

We waited. And waited. The disgust on Velia's face, her disappointment, became obvious. Velia finally fell asleep, and hard enough that Tages carried her to their bed. He returned, a line between his brows.

"Truly?" he asked, softly, nearly a whisper. "You see nothing different?"

"No. Everything is a bit louder, images a bit clearer, but not really much more than usual," I admitted.

"Louder?" he asked.

"Like when you overhear a conversation while reading and turn your attention to it."

"No ancestors?"

"Not mine. Just the Tree, an echo of two goddesses. No. Not even after you called them again and gave me more of the mushroom. Only the Tree. The one with the flowers I brought back. That's it."

"We'll try again some other time," he said. "You need to dream of your ancestors, to be part of a community, a lineage. Perhaps you will after this. You will let me know? Adepts need that skill."

I was disappointed, but could only accept. Maybe I wouldn't have a lineage, being a foundling. Maybe being exposed in the woods to die left me without ancestors.

Aule arrived the next afternoon, bringing not only a great deal of mud but a wagoner. They were filthy to their knees, and were splattered even on their shoulders from the wheels whenever they'd taken their turn to walk beside or behind the wagon.

"It's a miserable time of the year for travel," said Aule apologetically as I mopped up mud. His statement was echoed in the grumbles and tired faces of the wagoner and his boy. Even the mule looked exhausted, and whatever stubbornness it might have had had faded. Even I could lead it with a small bit of kindness.

We put everything in the hut, leaving most in boxes, but checking them. Only a few glass jars had broken. There were plenty of oddly shaped bottles, containers of some kind of burning fuel, copper pipes, pots, and books.

"Sen will unpack them," said Velia. "Suitable for an *apprentice*." She would not hide her disappointment.

"Mother, there's no reason to unpack anything without being able to set anything up. Tomorrow will do."

Her face was expressive in her frustration. "Well, the wagoner and his boy need a place to sleep. Sen, could you just arrange it better, then?"

"Of course," I said. I did this and retrieved bathing supplies and then took myself off to Tages's workroom, where I hid and read a book.

The next day, Tages, Aule, and I unpacked everything. Tages was focused on the essentials, not the rest. Aule helped me create some extra shelves for the extra equipment out of some of the supply crates, and as he set things up, he talked to us about the equipment.

"So, I brought fuel; it's in that metal canister. Often, candles will do for some chemistry experiments, but some distillations require a higher and longer burn," he said. He carefully moved the tins of fuel. He showed me the box with wicks and lids that could thread the wicks and also adjust them.

"What are these?" Tages asked, holding up two narrow glass tubes with something wound inside them.

"That one is a fracturing column, and this one is a condensing unit." He took a rounded glass jar, set it on one of the metal bases, then attached the fracturing column above it and then the condensing one fit at an angle. "This will allow you to have the extracts distill into the jar below it," he said, placing an open vessel below it.

He straightened, shrugged, and said, "I don't know how much use it will be for you, but the university offered it. Right now, it isn't a great season for it, being too wet. You can do a great deal without these, and I have that equipment as well. It can help distill wine into brandy for tinctures."

Tages shrugged. "Teas and pastilles work well enough for now."

"But a tincture being stronger could help Ravantha, don't you think?" I asked. "Easier to transport."

"From what I read, it takes longer to make."

"They also last longer in storage, and you don't have to wait for a plant to be in season, or lose potency over winter," said Aule.

"My apprentice will have to learn it then," he said, and began rummaging through the boxes of books. He took one and wandered back to the main house. Aule and I finished unpacking the boxes and organizing the space.

"Apprentice?" Aule asked.

"I didn't see anything different when I had the mushroom."

"Ah. No wonder my mother is upset." He paused. "You're not defective. I didn't either, but then I never really wanted to be a Doctor-Diviner. I did want to learn more about alchemy and chemistry, and, well... science. Without being able to see the world as my father did, but still wanting to help people one day. It was my best choice."

"You have no regrets?"

"No, not really. My mother's cooking, but not the rest of it. I would like your help with something. Professor Cuintus is intrigued by what we've studied with my father and what you studied with Turani. Will you help? He wants to learn of the herbs that you seem to know only in Ndeb."

"What would we be working on?" I asked.

"Proper Doctor-Diviner herbalism. Not the... adept or

Diviner work. That's too mystical for the university, regardless."

"I have been creating a reference for my own work," I said.

"I know. I like how you've been writing some of the Ndeb down. I was wondering if you would help me with some of that, and so I could extend my own learning in chemistry to isolate the compounds that make the plant effective in what it cures."

"That could be... interesting," I admitted. I put more bottles on the shelves, and carefully put some droppers into a small basket. "I have been thinking of taking my notes and creating a comparative Ndeb and modern taxonomy book, as a reference. Maybe I've already done something that would help you?"

"I'd like to see that."

I brought out my journals and we sat at the table, and he looked them over.

"These are your notes?" he asked. "Father didn't really need me or Cai to make journals like this."

"I had gathered that. I have, perhaps, gone beyond Tages's requirements. This is my own personal study."

Aule nodded, reading. I went back to unpacking boxes.

"I will admit that I did take it a bit further than what your father wanted. I was enjoying exploring and taking notes from what I understood."

He did not notice my words this time. He continued to read.

I unpacked and kept forcing my breath to steady, my hands to not tremble. I had spoken of this before he'd left, and now I wanted to know if he could see what I had. It had seemed as if something had opened up in the fall, before the winter, and now ideas were coming up as blossoms before their full bloom. My mind in its own spring.

Ndeb and proper herbalism and other components for our healing art had been fading in the studies of those who ought to have been our equals. Aule had confessed that he'd not been able to deny the ridicule rained down upon most of our colleagues. We all, pretty much, joined in.

Science, we suspected, would one day hold sway over Medicine; the trend would not help my career.

One idea that had come to me over the winter had been growing. It was to collect and detail plant life with the taxonomy of botanical science, but also in Ndeb—an idea becoming clearer, more detailed, but possibly unwieldy in perhaps going too far. I needed guidance. The rich, dying language of Ndeb could potentially be useful to scholars, as the language hid much lore in its words.

I had not shared this idea with Tages yet. Not fully.

My journals were, in fact, a combination of Ndeb with the herbalism and physiology underlying much of it, and the taxonomy of Aule's university science. Science supported what I had learned from Grandmother Turani, and what Tages was teaching me—even while we watched the underlying basis for our Medicine fade from use.

I almost dropped a small vial when he spoke, and I put it down and turned to him as he spoke.

"I really like this," Aule said. "Your observations are interesting. I think my father ought to look them over. This has more detail than I think he has observed. It is university-level work, and work I would be proud to do for my elevation-level work."

"He has seen them," I said.

"Yes, but has he *read* them?"

I didn't understand the question. I shrugged, not knowing what else to say. I opened up another box and pulled out two small metal buckets that fit together. The smaller one had holes in it. "What is this?" I asked him.

"Oh, one of the dehumidifiers for your tincture and oil cabinet. There's another in one of the other boxes, since it is the rainy season. That one you're holding is for salt. But charcoal works as well, and you have that with the fireplace. Either will draw moisture out of the air, helping keep mold out of your samples, tinctures, and oils. Oils, especially herbed oils, can get moldy."

He stood up from the table and rummaged through another of the boxes. "This one is for charcoal. The salt one, you'll have to dump water in frequently, but it works. I would still wait for a less wet season."

"How interesting," I said.

"There are others, but I haven't studied that much chemistry yet. Different substances made by combining different elements. I hope to bring you some of that one day, something that works better than salt. I'd like to understand it first."

The next few days, he talked me through some of the processes. He did have one precious jar of distilled water, and another of brandy, till I could make more for Tages's lab.

He walked me through making a tincture of some fresh spring herbs. I nursed the fire and pot overnight.

"You'll be able to compare water and brandy tinctures for their efficacy now," he said. "Steam distillation will help in making essential oils and stronger tinctures."

"I like this. Do you think I could use it for my private

comparative study?" I said.

"I don't see why not. The knowledge of how herbs in Ndeb work can have the same scientific testing as anything else. In some ways, there are people who might understand the world of spirit, but never be able to reach it."

Aule and I discussed the information for the paper we could work on. Aule had a professor who would oversee the chemistry side of things. He believed Professor Cuintus would be happy to oversee the botanical side of this paper. "He worries that you'll never get the accolades you deserve." I assured Aule that the height of my expectations was to one day gain my Mastery as long as I could continue my studies.

Privately, I could not picture myself in the Great City, at a university, or gaining a half-measured scholarship through marriage. Besides, my current work was better served by speaking with only the other person I knew who spoke Ndeb.

We had been sending Aule a great many herbs, as well as extracts made with our less advanced equipment. They helped pay for this new equipment, as well as a great many books. I now had books on plants and animals, and other kinds of books on biology and taxonomy. Tages pored over many books and Aule's notes detailing a great many new inventions.

There was a great telescope in the city he had seen. Farming near the city had undergone some innovation. More than just the plow he'd brought, there were threshing machines. He talked of any manner of invention, including matches and other objects that caused or used fire. The news was tantalizing, if strange and sometimes scary.

I scrubbed the walls of my hut with vinegar regularly to get the black stain off the otherwise pristine walls. I despaired. I spent too much time in the small hut, with a stifling fire drying out the room, along with the burners for steam-distilled essential oils and other extracts. I worked on sketches of the plants I'd gathered before the rains, and made notes about the properties I knew of, from their classification within Ndeb, as well as the modern taxonomy. For once in my life, and with so much time on my hands, I found myself thinking of other things.

I drew the Tree rising above the three chimneys. I didn't put that in my journal, but cut paper from old journals. I already had a few drawings—among the first I'd drawn from memory, not observation.

Tages came in as I was drawing one morning.

"That is the acropolis of the old city. The temple ruins."

"You know it?"

"Yes. When last I was there, however, the Tree you draw was not there." He picked up one of the other drawings. "It is not a Tree I know."

"You know so many plants. Perhaps I could take you to see it, and you'll recognize it?"

"Perhaps. Considering how well-grown it is, I wonder if I *would* see it."

"Excuse me?" I asked. "How would you not see it?"

"I was not there so long ago that I'd have missed seeing that Tree. It would have been far and away larger than a sapling unless it was incredibly fast-growing. I wonder at your not doing well with the mushroom. With Aule's pressing, I've reread some of your notes, and I'm beginning to wonder if you naturally see things, at times, that others do not."

I shook my head. It was a surprise. "How do I know what people do see or don't see?"

"You have almost encyclopedic knowledge of plants. It is why I value your counsel during Medicine. You are learning more about illnesses. It is why I think there may be an option for you to become an adept. Why do you draw this place?"

"Cai and I found this place when I escorted him home. I think this is where Grandmother Turani found me."

"It is possible."

"What else do you know of this ruin? Do you know its history?"

"When gods were men and inspired legends and myth, this was a place of gold and trade. The area was far wealthier than it appears now, all run to cattle and wildlife and trees. Even while the great god cities around the vast center lake of Obrone stood strong and mighty, this was outside that great ring of glory and rivaled their wealth. Despite Aule studying in a city called Jambrone, in those days, Jammon had no city. He was only the son of one of the greats. Divinity and his city came later. In the time of legend, it was in *these* ruins where Jammon found the gold before greed emptied the mine. Trade was good and went far and wide. Even to the south, and far to the north, overseas, and through danger. He bought the jewels and crafted the great necklace of Thielle."

I thought of how Grandmother Turani had talked of the story. It was almost as if she'd been there. I wondered at how different people thought of myths. How real were they to them?

"So he was a man, not a god? The craftsman, not the blacksmith?"

"Here he was a jeweler. I heard him described as more of a blacksmith in other parts. Sethlans, and not Jammon. Many of our legendary gods are heroes of the past. And so alike are some of the stories that they merge and shift, and some legends interchange. They indeed walked this earth, but if they were men or gods, I could not tell you. One legend says that to melt the metal to craft this necklace, he burned the wood of one of the daughter trees of the One Tree that is the umbilicus of the world."

He paused while I wondered if it was a sin among the gods to do such a thing, but then, we had drums made of sacred wood to help transport our minds to where the Spirits could hear us in our Medicine and even some of our divination. But crafting something that spoke as a drum was different from destroying the wood by fire.

"That seems legendary," said Tages, "But then, here you are drawing a Tree I cannot see." He tapped the drawing in his hand and put it on the desk.

"Ravantha said that Thefare has Thielle's necklace. I think Ati claimed it was the inspiration for her gold necklace. Is that true? That he has it?" I asked, knowing I had seen it.

"He has part of a necklace that is ancient. That I know. Whatever divine properties it has been said to have, clarity or healing, I see no signs of it. It is a thing. Maybe broken or too old for power."

"I know that Jammon chose Nhor over her sister, Thielle, and that Thielle wept." I raised my hands to the ceiling and the sound of rain on thatching. "The Apatin showed his fury in sending more rain so Jammon would never forget what he'd done. That is the gods' tale. What happened after? That is to the man, the jeweler."

I thought of that dream I'd had, of an event that had caused so much pain. At least one person thought the necklace must be of divine making, and worth enough to be part of

Ravantha's bride gift in exchange for valuable land. Was it merely a necklace, old and rare, made by a man? Then why dream about it, with something more akin to a Diviner's sight? If divinely made, then I could understand that a man might value it above profitable property.

"The story of the gods is a different tale, and his part rarely told," Tages said. "The story of the man Jammon is that he boarded a ship and disappeared to the east to the lost lands. He had to escape the wrath of the sisters' father and mother, and all the gods aligned with them. There are also stories that he consoled himself with a growing interest in alchemy."

"Which can rise from metallurgy," I said.

"Yes, and which is also the father of chemistry, without the problematic imagination—if it is such a thing—of magic."

I nodded. Magic had little to do with healing or divination. Tages deplored magic as being *outside* of nature, or an *attempt* to go outside of nature, including spiritual nature. His interest in science was because it allowed his own study to go far deeper than it could have otherwise.

"What happened to Nhor?" I asked. "If Jammon was a man, was she a woman?"

He shrugged. "The gods' tale says she was blessed with grace and hope. Well, depending on the region. In the oldest tale, I found, one helped protect life, the other to protect the dead. But I believe the story of the man and woman—and gods, as well, mingled in mystery—perhaps she sent him away, and spurned the gift he gave her? It is not in any temple, if the necklace in Thefare's treasure room is Thielle's or Nhor's."

"This is something I've wondered for some time. Who is the God or Goddess of Healing?"

"Do you know, I'm not sure. It could have been Thielle, in one of her aspects, or Tuvath, perhaps, the wife of the Apatin." He seemed to stop short, as if he'd never considered that problem.

Was the art and use of the Doctor-Diviner's role and purpose fading just as much as the long-forgotten deity of healing? Did the old colleagues pray to that divinity for aid? Was this part of why the craft was fading? Why Tages, I had to admit with a guess, struggled so? He interrupted my thoughts, almost dismissing my question.

"It is time for your lessons," he said. "Let me see your sketches and tell me of the plants you found. They are ready, I hope, from your press?"

"Yes. It's been a few weeks. I've kept them from the damp of the hut, and nearer the fire, but not so near to damage them."

"Good."

We spent the early hours going over drawings, notes, and plants from the press that were ready. I was able to tell him where and how I found most of the plants on my journey. Talking with him this way was the only thing that made me believe that there was hope. I forgot how hard I stood against the strange and growing pressures surrounding me.

There were rare moments when Tages and I talked, and I felt an echo of the strange power of time, like being and talking with Grandmother Turani. As if I could see not merely the turning of the world toward the sun, but the movement of age upon age, and a long line of history and legend and lore to the moment of now, like a thread in our hands. It generally happened when we were between experiments or studies. We used mainly Ndeb, but also spoke Obrone. I felt it now, but like the veins pulsing under my skin.

We were within the movement of an age, between one and the next.

It was strange that it also felt like any other day of instruction. He bent toward my book and examined the drawing. He suggested ways for me to draw plants to help others identify them more accurately. There was, to be honest, little that he could share with me at this point about the plants themselves, but changing the way I drew plants could be useful for the future. They need not be accurate as to the original, but must show specific items to help classify them within families. We discussed which plants we wished to study further.

"I like this. You should expand on this further. Even if I cannot make you an adept, this is worth equal to that."

"So, an adept without being an adept."

He shrugged. "You cannot get a degree in a university as Aule might, since they do not admit women, but if you cannot see what you need to see, how can you divine? I could not elevate you."

He gripped my shoulder, and I hid my disappointment.

"I do think this is valuable. What you might do with it, I cannot tell you. It is very good."

I smiled at him, feeling some sense of relief. It meant, in some cases, bringing plants to our strange garden, or wild-crafting the herb, that is, gathering it from the wild.

"We will have to gather more after the rains," he said.

I nodded.

"Or, rather, *you* will, as I have more work to do with the villages. I will also ask that you go back to the ruins. I am curious about that Tree."

"I'll be glad to go."

He paused. "I may have you stay with Ravantha for a time. She would like to get to know you better."

I shook my head. "There's no proof beyond chance that I am her daughter," I pointed out. The resentment I'd felt all my life toward thinking of *parent* did not rise. I stifled the shudder that she was, regardless of whatever truth there might be, making me into an image she preferred, not accepting me as I was. "There isn't, is there," I stated firmly.

"True. I'd hoped the adept test would confirm it one way or another. However, you were found within days of her daughter's birth and exposure. As a Doctor-Diviner, and with Velia helping with many births in this area, we kept records. Unless you were exposed by some person traveling far off the paths, I know well enough that there were no pregnancies as far along as Ravantha's. If you had been born early, you would have died."

This depressed me.

"Velia also tells me that Thefare is interested in you as well, as his kin. She seemed very interested in this. As she pointed out, if you were who they expect you to be, then not being able to even become an adept Doctor-Diviner does not mean your future is empty of purpose."

"And what would *he* want with me?"

"That I do not know, but considering his history, or your father's, it's bound to be less benign than Ravantha's yearning for motherhood. During these wet weeks, I'd like you to go to her and spend time with her. I do not know if you have any of the Diviner talent needed for an adept, but you have knowledge, and we can expand on that. Observe her. I am interested in what you might note. Later, we shall see about Thefare. I wish to know more about what their thoughts are. It can be good for us to have the attention and support of the lords of the land."

"Even when they are of different lands?" I asked.

"Of course. I am a Doctor-Diviner and have my own land, outside Thefare's control. Velia is right to be unhappy about this. I bought my land, and I could sell and chart another path, still of my own. Regardless of my agreements with him. I have reasons to stay."

He looked at my face. "Do not despair. You are *my* apprentice—and as such, under my protection. They have no claim on you except, perhaps, blood."

"*Possible* blood. If they'd put me in Turani's hands, then I'd say yes, I'm her daughter."

"Even so, you were sworn to me as my apprentice by the only person who claimed you. Blood can't change that. You grow in beauty and grace as Ravantha. It is possible you are her child, among many other equally unprovable possibilities. How can you determine you are *not* hers?"

I said nothing. He was right to suggest it. There was no proof either way. I rejected it, thinking: *Because I did not want her? Because I did not trust her?*

I was willing to entertain the idea that I was woefully naive about people and family relations. What Cai had said in early spring was correct. If I should resent anyone—were I that daughter—it was her father, not Ravantha. Could her painful attention toward me form a basis for love? The love of a mother and child? Would I know it if I had it?

If I had a choice to spend time with either of my supposed kin, my first choice would be her. I trusted my *uncle* even less and despised the man who could be my father by all this speculation. I dreamed of his attack on Ravantha each night before she'd arrive—

and her visits were not planned. I tried not to let those nightmares influence me, but there was a sense of compassion I felt for her... mingled with absolute rage I felt for Fuluns and Thefare. Till she showed up and looked at me with such hunger in her eyes.

"Well, it is time for our regular visit to Thefartown. Are you ready?"

"Are Velia and Aule coming?"

Tages shook his head. "No. They are catching up on the time they have missed with each other." He broke off with a chuckle. "Velia is trying to divine which of the women Aule knows in the city would be the best choice for him to wed."

Chapter Ten

⟪•⟫

On our walk into town, Tages was feeling cheerful. Whatever insight I might have, the work we did in town, without ceremony, rarely required it. We cared for minor illnesses and cuts and scrapes, and looked for illnesses that needed greater Medicine. We usually spoke Ndeb, instead of Obrone, when discussing patients. For them, it must have given our visits a more ritualistic coloring, and we knew that belief aided healing.

Tages was glad to have an umbrella to protect him from the rain. It was a gift from Aule and would certainly distinguish him from even Lord Thefare. I merely wore a hooded cloak, keeping our potions and herbs dry in front of me, hunching over them in the steady downpour. Tages carried the more expensive potions. The umbrella, however, did not protect him from the wealth of mud we slogged through. He was filthy up to the knee by the time we made it to the Great Market Court, and the hem of his once-white tebenna was splattered with mud and wet. It didn't matter. He'd take it off when we started working, and don the pristine tunic he'd kept safe in one of his bags.

Because of the rain, we didn't put any Doctor-Diviner paint on our faces, trusting our clothes would be sufficient to mark us as who we were. Besides, by now, surely we were familiar to anyone who might come for aid.

The Great Market Court was one of the few traditional buildings in the region that didn't have a round shape. It was open on all sides, but rectangular. Thefare's castle loomed over it, from a completely different vantage than the Women's Compound. The castle's more modern elegance—outdated, by Aule's description, as well as put to shame by Ravantha's own house—made the Market Court, and its hewn beams and shingled roof, seem both rough and ancient. This structure was possibly one of the oldest in the area. Having seen the ruins of Jammon's city, I could see how great the trees of the area must have been, for nothing in the immediate area had trees quite this large.

We spoke with and helped a great number of people. Scrapes, eye infections, coughs, headaches, and so on were among the most predominant problems. Tages and I spoke Ndeb to alert each other about things we needed to pay attention to, which might become greater illnesses or greater trouble in the future.

I suddenly realized I'd not seen him with his threshing basket, divining possible problems we might encounter. I realized I had not seen him use it in some time.

I wondered about this, but I'd been taught with other tools as well. Observation was an ever-practical tool that often looked to others like divination. Without Cai, observation was all we had. Certainly, all I had. This was food for thought. It explained, perhaps, why Velia was so unhappy with me. How often had Cai been doing the divination for Tages? And I unable to learn!

A number of people came to visit us, including Kutu's wife, Mawima, who wanted something to help her with her nausea, as she was pregnant with a new child. Tages came over to us and congratulated Mawima before returning to his patient.

Tages and I said nothing about her name. I tried hard to stifle my grin, even if she believed it to be about my happiness with her current state. But her name was too appropriate to the moment. It was from a Ndeb word for *ripeness*, one of the few names still given to women in the area that was not superseded by more popular Obronian names. I gave her a few teas to help her nausea, as well as to fortify her.

"Tell Kutu we are happy for you both!" I said.

"I will. He is pleased I can give him many children. He said he will bring you some pheasant when he can."

"Velia loves pheasant," I said. "As do I."

Tages grinned at me and started to make Ndeb and Obrone puns about ripeness and pregnant women. Our cheer had to be stifled because there were more sicknesses and minor injuries to tend.

It was late afternoon when we finished. I was beginning to pack up our things, and Tages was considering going to join some men at an inn for some wine—a rare outing for him—when two ladies from the castle compound approached—Arntlei to speak to Tages, and Hastia to speak with me.

"She wants to know when her husband will be back," Hastia said to me.

"Oh?" I turned to Tages and asked him in Ndeb, "Do you need me, sir?"

The woman was excited, but I could not be. I hoped Tages

would not want me, because I could not school my face.

He shook his head and replied in the same language. "No. It's a simple matter. Go and run the errands Velia asked about before we left."

I thought that with Hastia, she would not be too concerned by the sourness of my expression if I let that mask fall. She might be glad to see her father. I would not be. For Ravantha's sake. My own? Was her father my father? I tested that thought like tonguing a sore tooth. With distaste, I wondered if Thefare would end the banishment of his brother.

"Hastia! It is good to see you," I said. "How are you? How is Casiea?" She had been born in a poorer section of town. I wondered if she was still lonely after her parents died from a sickness born from polluted water. Perhaps Hastia kept her too busy to mourn.

"We are both well! I am to have my Milk Tree celebration!"

I was surprised. It was still a season of rain. How in the world would Arntlei manage that?

I stood up to take her hands into mine. "I am so happy for you," I said. "I have errands to run. Perhaps you can tell me about it along the way?"

There were few merchants in town that had not come to the Great Market Court, as they had their own buildings from which to sell their wares. Velia had requested I gather a few things. I had memorized the list. I had to run the list in my mind several times to be sure—some were rare food items—Velia was making an effort for her son, who she presumed had better access to these things in the city; others were for cloth, as being indoors and out of the rain gave her opportunities to sew.

Here I struggled. I could not remember the price Velia was

willing to pay, and the merchant's price seemed so high. Hastia stepped forward and took over the negotiations. She helped me bargain for a better price than I would get on my own.

"My mother has taught me a great deal," she said. "She generally does the bargaining. Thank you for giving me the opportunity."

I did not tell her that generally we got much of our wealth in trade, but this merchant's family had been quite healthy for a while. The bulk of the fabric was wrapped in oilcloth, so I could get it home without it getting wet. We had the package sent to the pavilion, leaving my hands free for the rest of the items on the list.

Hastia continued to tell me of the upcoming ceremony. "Velia is to come be part of the dancers. She is such a beautiful dancer, and that makes me excited. It will be beautiful, my celebration."

"Yes. She is a talented dancer," I said. Velia would do more than just dance. She was one of the few women who knew how to conduct the full ceremony. "I cannot wait to see her dance again."

Hastia shook her head. "Velia thinks that you should not be there for that part. We are of similar age, and you have not been celebrated as a woman yet."

I grit my teeth behind a smile. "I am still bound to my master," I said. "I understand."

"Will you help comfort my mother for those three days?" she asked. "Casiea is too young to comfort her and will be with the children."

I sighed and nodded. "When is it to be?"

"Two days hence, during the full moon."

"In this weather?" I asked, for it was still the raining season.

"Oh, we'll have it indoors, at the castle."

I nodded. I wondered at the rush, but shrugged my shoulders. Out of season, indoors, but only *true* women were allowed? It was traditionally done while the moon was waxing, and then completely full, with another day of its wane. We approached the Market Court, and I placed the items I carried on a table. Hastia's mother rose from her chair, happy, and gathered Hastia to her, and they quickly made their way to the Women's Compound with a quick goodbye.

"Hastia asked me to comfort her mother at the wax of the full moon."

"Ah! The ceremony, of course." He then went on to mention that it was partly because of the symbolism of the white, milky color of the moon in its fullness that they had the ceremonies at the proper moon. "It's also so that people can see to dance at night around a tree, and not bark their noses on some branch," he added dryly.

I laughed at that. "Not that it's needed here," I said. "As it's all to be indoors. In Thefare's castle."

Tages shook his head. "I am not surprised. Hastia refused to marry without one, and his negotiations with a land chief to the south are far too lucrative for him to pass on it. He would prefer a compliant, eager girl to hand over than one sullen and balky."

"But is the husband looking for a wife who knows her mind, is independent?" I asked.

Tages raised an eyebrow. "What kind of girl do you think Hastia is?"

Shrugging, I said, "I hardly know her. Spirited, I'd guess, but considering her cosmetics, and some of the brief chats we've had since discovering the outbreak of kolephera... romantic."

"That's perhaps the only answer her betrothed might need."

However irregular her menses, it didn't mean she couldn't bear. She was, at least, old enough to not risk her health. I was rather sad, though. Besides Cai, she was the only person I could consider a friend. If she moved south, I'd never see those coltish limbs blossom into womanhood.

It was the first of Milk Tree celebrations I had been able to attend, even if only on one side of the festivities and ritual.

Velia had lectured me about what would happen as we walked to the compound. I was grateful, for all I knew was theory. "You must let Arntlei mourn. If she doesn't, then the ritual will have no point."

She told me that the ceremony was being done around a chosen tree planted in a large urn.

"But isn't it too early for that?" I asked. "And isn't it going to be indoors?"

"Yes, but while it's to be done in Thefare's castle, it will also be in one of the great rooms. The seedling tree is in a pot, so she can take it with her," said Velia. "They do not have Milk Trees where she will be going."

"That makes sense," I said carefully. To my mind, the ceremony was edging toward the farcical.

"Thefare didn't think the ceremony was necessary, but

Hastia pressed for it, and Ati and I agreed it was necessary. We cannot give up all the old ways. I will see that it is properly done, even if indoors."

"I don't doubt. I hear her uncle has negotiated a match for her?"

"Yes. Her betrothed will be coming to see her soon," Velia said with a self-satisfied smile I could not understand. It was not her daughter who was being wed. Her friend's daughter, however, was making a rather advantageous match.

I nodded. "Do you know when?"

"In the month of the young hunt."

"Ah. So, she will be wed that soon, then?"

"Perhaps it is all too early. Hastia is barely large enough to nurse babies—except in age. The man might have thought to wed later in the year, but we can ensure that he doesn't get her belly up too soon. We must also wait for Hastia's father to return. He is coming. Thefare can only do so much knowing that Fuluns is still alive."

"Oh, that is surprising news," I said.

Velia shrugged. "That is news best kept to yourself, my girl," she said. "It will pain those we would like to comfort."

I knew she was thinking of Ravantha. I certainly wouldn't inform her.

There were no men present in the Women's Compound, only boys. Even Velia's cousin had been evicted from his house for this first night. Many women gathered in the main courtyard. Arntlei and Hastia exchanged clothes—as if they had died to each other. I had been to many funerals, where people wore the clothes of their dead, so as to have a part of them near as they mourned. A gesture of honor and respect, as well as deep grief, which gave meaning to the distribution of that person's material wealth.

It was strange to see Velia wearing a bodice as rich as Arntlei's or Ati's. I could also see that it was new. If she'd tried to hide it, it was revealed when she had to help Hastia into her mother's bodice. It was far too loose, and Velia had to undo the ties and wrap them around the girl twice. It was clumsy and awkward, but it had to do. Hastia's loose robes covered her mother but showed her ankles and forearms. The sight was incongruous and painful, adding to the real awfulness of the symbolic scene.

With clothing exchanged, Velia, in her robes and fashion, led the other women to hide Hastia. Through the growing crowd of women between us, I could see Velia taking the suddenly scared girl in hand and drawing her away.

Arntlei cried out, reaching for her daughter, wailing as if her daughter had died.

It was no act. She wanted her little girl. I held Arntlei back. She wept and told stories about Hastia as a baby. Velia had forbidden those who stayed with the mother to even mention that when it was all said and done, Arntlei would have a woman in her household, not a supposedly helpless child. She must mourn the child she would never see again.

I thought of the news Velia had shared on the walk while I comforted Arntlei on the loss of her daughter. And all my thoughts of that subject—her husband or Ravantha—were not something I'd begin to mention while I consoled Arntlei as she mourned the loss of her baby girl.

"She is so young!" Arntlei wailed. "Her father never had the joy of seeing his baby smile!"

"That is tragic," I said with as much conviction as I could

muster.

"But he will come soon!" Arntlei said. "He will come soon. His son will soon be of age."

So, Velia's supposition that Fuluns would come had the ring of truth here and more than for a wedding of a girl-child. Thefare could stand for his nephew, but the boy's ritual required his father—if his father was living. The upcoming season of hunting was the time when they gathered all the boys for their initiation ceremony. All the boys of a similar age had their initiations at one go.

Here, women were regarded as special—if they chose to have this initiation, or their mothers chose. Each girl had three days of their very own to celebrate their initiation, where they earned the full rights of becoming a woman. If they had the ritual at all.

I wondered what Ravantha would make of Fuluns's return. If I were her daughter, he would be my father. I wondered if the woman beside me knew who they thought I could be.

"I did not realize that Hastia had a brother."

"Yes, that boy there," Arntlei said. "Teitu."

"He looks like he will be a strong young man," I said. He had come in after all the women had left for the castle. He was at least quiet. I thought of his age and knew that Arntlei had met with Fuluns at least once since his brother had sent him away.

Arntlei wept, looking at her boy. "He has waited too long for his father to return. Thefare has sent for him."

None too soon, I thought. Of size, he was a young man, better built than his sister.

Arntlei started to cry again.

"Hastia's now gone! Soon he will be as well! My babies!

They all go away!" Arntlei wept at the thought of her children leaving. Teitu came over and patted his mother on the shoulder. "Don't cry, Mother," he said.

But she did. She held his hand and wept onto his arm. Teitu looked uncomfortable. He patted her on the head, and as soon as she let go of his hand, he backed away. "I'm going to go stand guard with my cousins," he said.

The boy fled. Even Cai would have fled when it was possible. No man likes a woman's tears. Cai, however, would have stayed longer and made tea to calm the hysteria. I held her as she wept with this new loss.

As soon as she calmed, I signaled her servant to comfort her and went to make tea. I used oat straw, rare in this region, as well as balm, both herbs good for hysterical emotions. When my back was turned, however, Arntlei started toward the door. I leapt toward her so fast, and held her, with her servants helping me settle her back down.

The servant worked on finishing the infusion while I held her and comforted her.

For Arntlei, the ritual was real. Her daughter, the little girl, was dying or dead. Their relationship would never be the same.

I sat with Arntlei for two more days as the ceremony continued and gained far more sympathy for Ravantha than I had had before.

When it was over, Hastia burst into her mother's house.

"Arntlei!" Hastia called out.

She would never call the woman *mother* now. She would forever use her mother's name. She was a woman now, and dressed properly like one, though rather modern. The bodice did what it could to emphasize what breasts she did have, and the cut and cloth told me this was part of her wedding clothes.

Arntlei leapt up, exhausted with lack of sleep and days of weeping, and held the young woman tightly. Only when they released each other did they greet each other more formally, as woman to woman. A purely formal and archaic greeting used in rituals like these. They did not understand the words in Ndeb, except as Velia had translated for them.

In my opinion, they could have said it all in Obrone, and it would still have meant something. But to Hastia, the Ndeb words had mattered. Without those words, they would not have what they did now.

The two women who held each other's hands were now nominally equal in each other's eyes. The community now acknowledged that Hastia was a woman in her own right and equal to her mother. No more a child. Two adult women stood and hugged each other.

Chapter Eleven

⫷◆⫸

The next day, I left to visit Ravantha, Tages wishing me to stay for some time. After I learned that Fuluns would soon be returning to the area, and had, in fact, probably visited more than once as he had a son old enough for initiation, I was almost glad. Time in the Westvell seemed appealing in comparison. I had no wish to meet a man who raped young women.

After some thought during my long walk, considering the attention I'd already received from Ravantha, Thefare's brother became even more disconcerting. My status as an apprentice was a shield. It was protection that felt flimsy enough. And yet... I wanted that growing autonomy. Working away from Tages's tutelage was, actually, adept work—without the practice of divination. I chaffed at this thought and cursed myself for not having passed Tages's test with the mushroom.

I thought to myself, *Let the Apatin's rain wash these evil thoughts away!*

Apprentice

Before I left for the Westvell, Tages and Velia ordered me to accept gifts from Ravantha. Velia was shocked when she realized I was not actually thrilled about the visit and had only agreed because Tages ordered me to go.

"You will not make a good Doctor-Diviner if you don't accept gifts," said Velia. "It is how we live."

I looked up at the cheeses I'd hung the day before, and thought of other items she and I had made in months past that more than amply funded the household. But if I were honest, with Tages more and more often holed up in his workroom, without visiting any of the surrounding villages, his contributions to the larder *were* certainly less. The household *needed* an adept. The only candidate was me. I couldn't see my ancestors, and so how could I call upon mine to aid my own healing, and thus understand how to do yet more to aid others?

Many people in the surrounding area knew they could call on Tages, but he did not work a circuit like he must once have done. Cai had done more of that during his adept days.

"Payment comes from providing a service. What service am I providing her?" I asked.

Velia practically yelled, "You *are* providing her with something, or she would not *want* you."

"I cannot pretend to be a dutiful daughter when I do not believe that I'm her daughter!"

"I'd prefer you put that aside, regardless," said Tages. "You will be observing her, as well as how she runs her estate and county —necessary information for your future, even just as a Doctor-Diviner you will hopefully be one day. Your observations on her health will be of great importance."

Tages handed me some stoppered gourds with clay, along

with some extracts in blown glass vials. "There are some things that need healing we cannot see—and Ravantha's illness is one of those, as physically healthy as she is. Her brain is wounded. You can admit that, correct?"

"Yes, Master," I said.

He raised his eyebrows and shook his head at my rare use of the term, though he was that to me.

"Sen, she is asking for you, and as my student, one can say she is begging for healing—even if not for her brain, but her mind. I ask you to go as my apprentice. See what you can learn without the divination you cannot do, and that most *doctors* taught in a university would never consider. Accept her gifts for what you can bring her. Do this as my student, and learn what you can," he said. "We could use her gifts. Thefare has seen enough of you, to my mind and... I divine something, but..." A strange look came over his face. "It is too vague."

Velia looked both stricken and thoughtful as he said this. She began to be agitated. Picking up tools, herbs, putting them down. I was embarrassed by their sudden tension.

I knew that implied in his words was "Take notes!" I sighed. That I could accept; if it was for healing, I was bound to accept any gifts she might offer.

"Give me the copy of Palecu's book on the anatomy of the brain," I said.

"Palecu is a thin read," Tages said, watching Velia leave the room.

When the subject became technical, she often went about her own pursuits. I heard her grumble, "Modern, spiritless, dead..." The words trailed off.

I said, "But it does list a great deal about brain injury, both bloody and not. And he's listed his findings on autopsies and prior symptoms."

"The living are not the dead," he said. "You cannot peel open her skull to peer inside."

"It gives me something to do! I'll take my journal of my studies on Vesalus as well."

"Sen, neither book is going to help you fix Ravantha's head. The damage is done."

"Of course not! I will, however, feel as if I'm there to study something. Not even Palecu has recorded or tracked the long-term effects of brain injury." I looked up at him and thought to myself, *This is close to adept's work*, and started to ask him about my elevation in rank, wondering if there was any other way to go about it, but he spoke first.

"True, and what you record will be important. There might be more for you to observe. Vesalus has started getting his students to record those effects, but Palecu seems to focus only on autopsy. I've already put paper in your hut, so you can pack it. If you have time, pursue your studies comparing Ndeb and taxonomy. If we are lucky, you'll have something to send to Cuintus when you come home. I'd like to see it first."

"Of course. You are my mentor and master, not Cuintus," I said. I did not say that it would be aggravating to study with Ravantha hovering over my notes. I would write them all in Ndeb.

I went and was, of course, bestowed with gifts.

I will admit that waxed, fitted leather boots were fabulous during the month of rain.

Ravantha's house was large, but fairly empty of people. She had few servants, though I quickly learned that she had far more wealth than Thefare, because her farmland was among the best in the region. Much of it was largely hidden from view, the main thoroughfares being within woodland. While I did not like her, it was clear that she managed her land adeptly. Thefare was a fool for refusing to give up a broken necklace for this abundant wealth I knew he craved. However far from Aranthenden, it made Aranthur's need for the necklace all the more curious.

I did not get to try my new boots out of doors all that often. It was wet still, more than it was not. I was not alone with Ravantha, which I counted as a blessing. Larce and Marce were visiting. They slogged through the showers that were still frequent, bringing in quite a lot of mud for Ravantha's servants to clean. I quickly discovered they were there by design. She wanted them to help train me to defend myself.

I refused to use a knife, or a sword, or even a bow.

She was shocked when it was clear that while I had accepted her gifts of leather boots and better clothes—I'd *known* it would set a bad precedent—I would not train with these sharp things. She had pressed, and, realizing I could not win, I had fled.

She tracked me down in my room. As usual. It was a retreat, and a bad one. I had yet to find a better.

"Why," demanded Ravantha angrily, "will you not listen to me and train with these men?"

There was a high-pitched tone to her voice, and she was vibrating with fury. I took note, wondering how much of her sentiment was fueled by her brain injury.

"I am being trained as a Doctor-Diviner," I explained as calmly as I could. "I do not want to cut into someone to defend myself. Have you cut into something that was once alive, or cut into something that is alive?" It was hard to speak gently. I was angry. She knew how I was being trained!

"No," she admitted, but she was clearly still agitated. "But who cares about Doctor-Diviners anymore?"

I gawped at her. "You do! You get Tages's tinctures and teas and medications regularly."

She snorted, and I felt waves of something that might have been horror, might have been shame.

"A glorified apothecary, closer than the physicians in Jambrone," she said, dismissing my life's work.

The words from a woman who wanted to be my mother were like a punch in the face. It rocked me back on my feet, so that I almost fell. Trying to damp down my sudden rage, I said as evenly as possible, "I do not want to learn how to fight. I can probably tell you quite easily where to kill someone with one blow—if Larce and Marce haven't already—but I will not cause damage *I* will have to heal. That I'll have to use thread and needle to sew up, in hopes that my own actions will not cause death. Because I'm bound to do so." I heard the tremor in my own voice, and I tried to breathe steady breaths to calm myself.

"And if someone is *attacking* you, what then?" she shouted.

My jaw clenched like a vise. I did not voice my thoughts, thank all gods. *I would not trust a strange man to get me into a room alone and unsupervised!* My own stomach turned so sour I could taste it, and I had to bite back bile. I was horrified at this unbidden thought.

The *only* person to blame was Fuluns, *not* his victim.

What she had said to me, which hurt so deeply, was probably close to the truth.

What I bit back from saying was not.

With deep shame, I stepped back from my anger,

swallowing bitterness.

Thinking of those dishonorable thoughts, I knew it had been words that would have been used as a weapon to fight back against those words she'd used. *Glorified apothecary.* I felt clammy. Thank all the gods, I hadn't said anything. Guilt made me nauseated; shame made me cold in my sweat. It did not matter one bit if *she'd* tried to embarrass me, or even Tages.

How would I know when a comfortable, seemingly safe situation was not? I was even *less* experienced than Ravantha had been at that age.

My jaw was still clenched in bruising force before I could speak those vile words, and before the bile in my belly could rise up past my throat. I was horrified by my own thoughts. Weeks of resentment had inspired no good thinking. I felt inadequate, inexperienced, and insufferable.

I watched her jaw clench, and I felt as if I was failing my mentor in the task he'd given me. My shame grew; I almost became dizzy.

Yet it illuminated as well. I knew something I had not known before; I did not know how to reach her. I *should* still be an apprentice if I behaved so badly. It was a hard lesson. Worse: I knew that I had not wanted to reach *this* patient, to understand her so that I could help her in even the smallest way. I would remain an apprentice all my life, in fact, no matter what titles were *ever* bestowed upon me, if I could not find it in myself to reach her even in some little way.

Beyond any doubt, I would never reach her fully. Yet I could make some kind of amends. I could make one step toward her to regain peace. Not merely between us, but for her.

I took a deep breath. I aimed for honesty.

"We are not communicating. We must both be feeling unseen and unheard. You think I trust easily. I do not. I do not trust you. I do not trust Thefare. I don't trust Marce or Larce. I do not want anything from people assuming a relationship for which we have no natural proof or natural trust. I also do not want to learn a skill contrary to my profession, one chosen for me by Grandmother Turani as being close to what she had taught me all my life. If you will not hear me, then I must leave, regardless of what my mentor has asked of me." I kept my tone as soothing as I would when treating a screaming, injured child. A tone that often worked to calm the child.

Ravantha seemed to respect the tone, and her shoulders relaxed, and the agitation on her face shifted into thoughtfulness. Shocked thoughtfulness, but we had at least come here, even as she trembled.

"You don't trust *me*?" This, apparently, surprised her most of all.

I didn't mention her insult to my craft. "You look at me with just as much planning and possession in your eyes as Lord Thefare. I don't know what *his* plans for me are, and I'm not sure what your plans are. Yet you both want to claim me without asking me what I think. Of course I'd be resistant. I let my own defensiveness lead me to thoughtless, hurtful behavior. I'm sorry."

To my surprise, she sat back and pondered me for a long while.

"What do you think?" she asked, finally.

"That neither of you has a claim on me," I said. "All the parent I needed was Grandmother Turani."

"So not even the great Tages is family?" However much she valued his medicines, her tone remained slightly derisive.

I told her the truth. "He is my *mentor*. He is my master. Not my father. I am his apprentice. I am not his daughter. I will gain adept status and then Mastery through him. I *respect him* and his work. I trust him as my teacher."

"What would convince you that you are my daughter?"

"I don't know."

"What about the gown I sewed for you? Your baby swaddling clothes. Part of Thielle's necklace was in my fist when they found me. I sewed it into your swaddling clothes as part of your future dowry. One day, I will have that necklace in Thefare's keeping, as I have you back now. I did not know my father would come and take you. But he did. When I knew he'd taken you, exposed you in the woods for the lions or jackals to take... I never forgave him. But he took you wearing those baby clothes I made for you."

I shuddered. What an awful memento to sew into an infant's first clothes! I trembled again, realizing she still refused to admit any doubt.

"I never saw them, Ravantha."

"But I did. I know you wore them. You have the leaf-like shape on your thigh similar to that silver pendant. I saw it when you bathed."

I shuddered. "You watched me while I *bathed*?" I did have a liver mark the shape of two leaves on my thigh. I had not made that connection to the necklace. Why would I? The gleam of hope that maybe I did have a family—surprising in how it rose up, unbidden and unexpected, making my heart pound—was dashed as I shuddered again. The thought of her watching me during my private moments was yet more disturbing. Whatever I represented to her was powerful, if not reality.

My throat choked again on rising bile. If her longing for her daughter was genuine, there was still something rather unbalanced here. I felt pity for her, which I tried to ease into compassion. I still felt too young, too inexpert.

"I wanted to make sure you were safe."

"From *whom*? There aren't any men who stay the night in your manor house."

"I cannot guard all the walls!" Her words were like a wail.

I was an apprentice Doctor-Diviner. We dealt with more than physical illness, but beyond depression, most of it was pure theory embedded in stories and lore. I heard a wealth of pain in her cry. Sewing gems that reminded her of rape into her baby's clothes was not exactly an idea formed by a rational mind. I wondered how she slept at night. How long had she been so hyper-vigilant? I could guess—my whole life, whether I was her daughter or not. Would she ever feel safe?

I had not truly thought either Palecu's book or notes on anatomy would really serve me here. The idea of studying her actions for brain injury had been more of a shield and reason to justify being here. I did not think she'd give me more cause to ponder the severity of symptoms incurred by her attack. I realized what Tages had meant with his request before I left. He had seen something I had not.

I had resisted noticing anything but that she irritated me. Tages might trust my *insight*, for whatever that was worth, but I had a great deal to learn. I now saw it, nauseatingly bare. My distrust of her had blinded me. I had reacted to her, not observed.

It didn't matter. This moment made me realize why I had no trust that *I* could help heal this woman. If anything, I made things worse. I could track and observe and ask maybe a few discrete questions to those who had known her longer. It would not help much.

I was disconcerting to the peace of her mind, as she was to me. Poor woman.

I would have to tell Tages that *if* healing in both mind and body were possible, I could not be the one to offer it; her thoughts about me were as unbalanced as thoughts of that broken necklace. She was more fixated on that than on any revulsion toward Fuluns, Thefare, or even her father—Fuluns had been at too considerable a distance. What would happen upon his return?

What she felt was some kind of glory in possessing either this necklace or me, as if she could gain proof of her personal power in possessing us. As if she could have power over what had happened to her. Even this many years later, I could understand why she might want that.

Were I to become the greatest Doctor-Diviner in all of Obrone, I could never truly heal her. So long as I represented her daughter, it would never happen. I would have to live beyond, be recognized beyond her framework of family. I prayed and wept inside my heart to the forgotten or lost Goddess of Healing.

I spoke on the only thing I had any potential say in while I stayed with her—my future training, or lack of training, in any martial art.

"Ravantha, I will not study to use a sword or something that will cut," I said.

I knew it wasn't enough, but it was a concession. It was the only thing I could do. It was the only way I could gain any kind of trust with her, or at least peace with her, while I stayed. One did not need blades to damage a person. Pictured in my mind was how Fuluns had beaten her head into the bricks of the treasure room. I knew how deep the damage of bruises could go. I suspected that physical trauma could extend the emotional one.

Thanks to Vesalus's and Palecu's books, I knew that the head need not be opened up to damage the brain. I saw it sitting across from me. Both men had clearly seen what generations of healers had not. If the skull stayed intact, for the most part, physicians, surgeons, and even Doctor-Diviners had thought the injury less, not potentially a great deal more. Blood and pressure could build inside a skull, and trepanning was still considered dangerous because of infection. I wondered if there were ways to improve upon that ancient art.

I yearned to talk with Tages more about lasting injuries to the brain and innovations in surgical aid. Trepanning had been something done in ancient times. Surely it could be done better now, even if far, far too late for Ravantha.

My learning to fight meant something to her. It was the only thing I could offer her.

"A staff or sticks, then?" she asked.

"Even my fists, if need be," I said, but I was not happy.

She perked up. She almost looked like one of Hastia's cousins in the market, chasing after ribbons. I shuddered at this dramatic, mercurial change. Tages had told me that for months after her head injury, impulsiveness had been extreme in Ravantha's behavior, as well as sudden tempers that amounted to fury. I could add mercurial shifts in emotion to my notes—written in Ndeb, clearly, as she had little respect for any of my boundaries.

"Come," she said. "You will feel stronger knowing how to protect yourself! I know it."

I stifled a sigh and followed—knowing that if I didn't, she'd take me by the hand and lead me like a child.

"She will learn staff," Ravantha announced. Even her demeanor had changed so dramatically, I could not help but suppress a shudder. "I'm so relieved!" she said.

I kicked myself, mentally. Merely because her injury inspired irrational mood swings, it did not mean that her feelings weren't genuine. The greatest fear she had was rape, and my being able to defend myself mattered. I realized it ought to matter to me.

"It is a good choice," Larce said.

It became interesting as a student Doctor-Diviner to train with weaponry. Not merely for the use of muscles which I was, frankly, glad to train. Without foraging or all my other work, I felt sluggish. I also took note of injuries, potential injuries, and how to heal them. Those of the Hunter Cult would, no doubt, need those kinds of healing. The time spent also gave me opportunities that Ravantha would not guess would interest me—that is, to observe her interactions with Marce. It was clear that they still liked each other. He was courteous. In fact, he showed greater respect for her personal space than she did for mine. I had a terrible fear that if given an opportunity, she would bathe me like a baby, the way she'd offered to comb out my hair—neither of which I ever let her do.

My days were spent mainly with the three of them, training with the staff, or riding Marce's horse, Achivizer, when the days were fine. I refused to explain why the name of the horse made me laugh. Clearly, he was not versed in legend or lore. In some legends about Thielle, she had a winged creature named Achivizer that was her attendant. Granted, Marce was a handsome man. He was not a goddess of beauty or love. But I liked him.

He did not like me, at first, in fact. As he grudgingly taught me, he revealed his reservations. He admitted I was a thinking person. "Not like those quacks and charlatans who prey upon my father," he said, as if this was enough information to explain his early coldness. It was.

I had surprised him by replying, "I've come across a few myself. I don't like them, either."

"My father prays for a healing that they refuse to give. My father now believes that only gods might heal him. So, he's an easy target for anyone with that sort of reputation, deserved or not. If they don't invite themselves, he solicits any who might be willing."

"I believe he consulted Tages," I said, wishing I knew the contents of that letter.

"Your mentor's answer did not suit him."

"What was it?" I asked. "My mentor did not share it with me."

"I don't know," he said. "He threw the reply into the fire and had a temper on him that lasted weeks."

I resolved to ask Tages about it when I had the next opportunity.

Larce seemed to relax more when I was there, as if he had more respect for my work than Marce had. He appealed to me for decoctions that might help with nerves a time or two. I could see that Marce's hand sometimes trembled. Other times, Marce seemed to stumble as if suddenly dizzy. I noticed that I was observing this and noting it before Larce did.

I ran my thoughts over the symptoms. I could tell that neither man overindulged in too much drink. The tremors must have other causes.

I began to observe him, adding it to my observations of Ravantha.

He was the only man I knew who speculated I could be

Ravantha's daughter who didn't appear to have plans for me. He just seemed glad that I trained well with the staff, though it was early days yet. It was among the few joys I had during those weeks. The other was his horse. I took to riding Achivizer as if born on his back.

There were times I wanted to walk off and leave them all behind. I did not, no matter how many times a day Ravantha provoked me or disturbed me. I had promised Tages.

Achivizer was deep black and seemed ridiculously intelligent. He seemed to always know what I wanted, such as when I wanted to go from a walk to a canter before I shifted in my seat. It was as if the horse could understand me better than those who supposedly cared for me. He also taught me to observe in ways I hadn't before. He was generally calm and so easygoing that it was almost as if he relaxed so that any change could be noted. Inspired, I worked to gain his composure. It was hard, with all the provocation.

Besides riding the horse, the only other entertainment I had was Larce and Marce's friendly competitions. Despite having Cai and Aule as companions at one time, I'd never seen this kind of teasing affection, with or without any sense of competition. They challenged each other to feats of strength—like climbing one side of the rock, which proved impossible for either, or how far one could slide in the slope of mud at one of the hilly paths in the village below.

"The challenge ought to be who overworks the servants washing or mending your clothes!" I said.

They laughed but were abashed. I wondered then if they played like this when they were home. There was a sense of joyous freedom the two men had here that one might hope they could have anywhere else.

Larce laughed less than Marce, but I'd already come to see that I was the only one noticing how often he was protective of Marce, even during these feats of bravery. Even his teasing while they climbed the manor walls pointed out better handholds. Marce still climbed that wall, but his friend helped him. Larce's joy —or relief—at any successful feat of Marce's was like the sun shining after a storm.

Ravantha reprimanded me for my criticism. "Once I would have been right there with them," she said. "So, they can muddy my floors any time."

It was clear that she could not or would not try to match some of their feats of bravery. The thought of her trying to climb the manor wall was impossible. I thought she could do it, but she was too afraid of headache. I tried, and they laughed at my efforts. It was akin to climbing a tree, which was a necessary skill when wandering in lion country; that is, if one could get high enough where the big cats could not reach. Lions were often good at climbing trees and clawing at them. Larce told me how the hand grips for stone were different from a tree.

"Useful when I was a lad, wanting to get out of the house and go running through the park in the moonlight."

Marce leaned over his shoulder. "Yes. Cultured garden that it was, his mother didn't realize there were plenty of places to hide. He set up pranks to tease his sisters." Marce grinned. "He used to get into so much trouble!"

"Used to?" I said.

"Well, I still get in trouble, but I'm a man grown. They cannot punish me *now*. Then, they wanted to punish me, but they couldn't figure out how I'd done it," Larce said with a laugh.

"Till one day we both went out, and he got scared by a bat and fell."

"I didn't even break an arm!"

"He fell into his mother's rose bushes and came away with only several hundred scratches."

"Don't forget the whipping my father gave me!"

The two men laughed at this.

"We behave now as seemly gentlemen," Marce said.

He saw the look on my face.

"Truly," Marce said with a laugh. "We have brothers who game in the cities, drink heavily, and carouse with women. His brother Lecen even became sick with that sort of thing."

Larce was pained by this, I could see. He shook his head. "It is difficult to realize that while I was considered the truly wild child, he's the one who might suffer the most, coming to it late."

"That is, unless you fall down a boulder or a manor house and break your neck," I said.

"No, Sen," Marce said seriously. "We test ourselves all the time, and our horses—which you might see if the weather was fine."

"But," Larce continued, as if they were of one mind, "we never hurt our horses. You can tell by their mouth. We've given over the recklessness of youth. We test our limits."

I knew what Larce said was true, but had either man fallen onto granite rock without a thornbed of rose bushes to catch their fall, they might have proven that while they weren't reckless, their games could be dangerous.

Larce continually watched his friend carefully. And I had begun to know why. There were too many times Larce took over teaching me after Marce had started because he could not hold his staff. He claimed he'd just hurt his hands. I noted how quickly Larce took over, and with such practiced grace as not to embarrass his friend, and to take the focus upon himself.

I knew I'd read about something like this, but could not remember what. Which was why Tages was the expert, and I was still an apprentice.

One day, when it was just misting with rain, the clouds low and gray, but not quite as angry as they could be in this month, Larce had me work with him in the woods, with Ravantha and Marce sitting on the hilltop to watch when they could. It was a mark of her trust in both men that she'd let me out of her sight while with him.

"You've been watching them," Larce said when we were out of earshot.

"She seems comfortable with him."

"She is."

"Will she marry him, then?"

"His wife and father would have to die first. Aranthur is the type of man to hold grudges and is infuriated by the whole thing still—especially as Marce has no child."

"For these many years?" I said, hiding my shock that Marce was actually married, and had been.

"Oh, well, I wouldn't worry on that count. Marce is content for many reasons—though there is no child to prove it."

"She knows he's married?"

Larce shrugged his shoulders. "It's no secret. As far as any future connection, at least Aranthur knows she is able to have children at one go. However old we are now, she's not past bearing by many years. Her father might not approve, but she's demanded her freedom to choose. It's possible she will remain single, even if

Marce becomes free. I do know that she plans her revenge on Fuluns, when and if the opportunity arises." There was a strange grin on his face. "And we support that plan."

"What is she going to do?" I asked.

He looked a bit surprised that he'd revealed that there was a plan. "I won't tell you. Maybe when you're an adept, you can divine it."

I thought Larce's answer was a bit strange. Why tell me this much, but no more?

I wondered then why both men visited so often.

Clearly, Marce and Larce had plans, even alongside whatever plans Ravantha had for getting her revenge on Fuluns. I would be content to not know more, not only because it disturbed me, but because I needed and wanted to believe that it had little to do with me.

"And you? Why are you here?" I asked Larce.

"Me? I'm quite capable of participating just for the mischief of the thing, and I will not be parted from my friend easily. Anything I do is for him and his future. If I had another reason, all I would say is that Fuluns didn't sully just one girl. He imposed himself upon someone close to me—and ran to the protection of his brother, who was, at the time, rich enough to protect him, and justify his actions—without recourse for the woman."

"That's terrible."

"She killed herself. Ravantha, at least, is still alive."

I shuddered. I had no doubt that Fuluns needed to be dealt with, but there was something in Larce's tone that I found troubling. The conversation left me feeling almost as exhausted as spending a day having Ravantha watch my every move.

It was also terrifying to discover that I had to watch my every word as well. One morning, I'd made a passing comment about my porridge being cool. Before I could say anything good about the flavor of the berries and spices, Ravantha flew into a rage. She took the offending bowl, stormed into the kitchen, and threw the porridge pot toward her kitchen staff. The cook stumbled into a fire to avoid the flying mess. I was horrified, and yet, Ravantha's quick movements prevented the woman from burning more. Even as the woman fell, Ravantha grabbed her and pulled her out, screeching in horror at what she had done. I ran forward and grabbed the skirts that were burning and worked to put the fire out. I ended up having some burns.

I sent someone to get my healer bag, and called another one to bring some milk as I cut away more of the cook's skirt, so I could see how far the burn had gone on her thigh.

"What is your name?" I asked her, as I carefully poured the milk over the burns of the poor servant—mine were far less—to cool it, without the harshness of water.

"They call me Ziia—Araziia."

"I'm sorry about this, Ziia. Some of it will hurt," I said, knowing the pain of it in my own hands. I kept my voice calm, working to bring the tension in the room into cooler draughts.

Ravantha cried. "I don't know why I get so mad sometimes!"

"You must control yourself, Ravantha," I said, still calmly. So that no one would see either grim lip or clenched jaw, I worked the muscles of my ribs to force my breathing to be slow. Still, I noted her symptoms as well as my more needy patient.

What I could see of it needed immediate attention. Most of it seemed angry and red, but no worse. I could ignore the gulping noise of Ravantha trying to control her remorse.

"My Lady," Ziia said, "You saved me from worse. I've never seen anyone move so quickly."

"Well, I'd rather your dress burn than you!"

"I'm sorry about the porridge."

I looked about. "I've never been here. I didn't know it was so far from the dining hall. It's incredible that any of your food comes to us hot," I said. "Who builds a kitchen a mile from a dining hall?"

She laughed, but there were tears in her eyes. The servant Mena had returned with my healer bag. I knew her better, as she usually served us in the main hall. I looked in my bag and found a salve Tages had made up. I also brought out the herbs for an analgesic that I was sure Ravantha would need before long. Fortunately, it would help Ziia as well.

"Mena, could you also brew a pot of this, strong?"

"For how long?"

"Steep for at least ten minutes. One cup for Ziia, and a large mug for your Lady."

Ravantha had already stopped crying and came near, wanting to help.

"She will need a clean dress," I told her.

She sent Mena off for clothing, but I amended that, seeing as it didn't make Ravantha leave—and said that Ziia needed a cool place to rest. Mena nodded. I turned back to my patient, and Ravantha watched me salve Ziia's leg. I was grateful to salve her, as my own hands had begun to sting from the burns on them.

"I had been about to ask what was in the porridge to bring out the mellow flavor of the berries," I said.

The servant looked at me, surprised. "Truly?"

"Yes," I said as I carefully put salve on the lesser burns.

"Your mother..."

"Not my mother for sure, Ziia."

Ravantha shook her head and gave one of her sweet smiles. "Don't worry, Ziia. It is an old argument between us," she told her servant. "Sen does not wish to be greedy, nor reach higher than her upbringing."

I tried not to roll my eyes.

"We used a seed called ilatchi, as well as some ground bark whose names I forget. The cook calls them aromatics."

"Well, they are very tasty with the berries and porridge."

Ziia smiled, and then winced as I started to get to the greater burn.

"This part of the burn," I said, "is too wounded for the salve. The heat of this burn needs to be free to rise from the wound. If I salve, it will keep the heat in, which will hurt more and slow the healing."

"Like a lidded pot that's come to boil too long, and dances?" she asked. "Sometimes you want the lid on, so the water comes to boil more quickly. But too long, and if the water is too high, it will dance and jump off."

I grinned at her. "Yes."

Mena came back, saying Ziia's room was ready. The infusion was ready as well, and she gave Ravantha a large mug of it.

"You drink that now," I told her. "As a healer, I can already tell one of your headaches is coming on," I said. "You need to go to a quiet room and rest."

"My head *is* beginning to hurt."

"Then you must drink it now, and then go rest," I said,

seeing that she was being mulish and not wanting to leave my side. "If you drink it and retire to your rooms, I will promise to look in on you when I'm done here," I said as if to a child. I felt my ribs ache as I forced my breathing to be slow and steady. She nodded, however, and complied.

Mena and I took Ziia to a room. We removed the rest of her burnt dress and put her in a light shift. After ascertaining that there were plenty more—though I would have given the woman some of mine at need—I sliced the shift so that Ziia's leg was exposed, but the rest of her body could be covered. We helped her drink her cup of tea. I stayed with her till she'd finished, and then left her to rest.

"I'll return to check on you," I told her.

"You're a lady. You should not take such notice of a servant!"

I shook my head. "Whatever Ravantha believes of me, I am an apprentice Doctor-Diviner more than anything else. It is my honor and duty to heal anyone who needs it."

"You are very good," she said.

I went back to the kitchen, where Mena was clearing the mess. I noticed that kitchen servants were returning—and that there were more than Mena and Ziia. I took the salve from Mena and finished tending my own burns. One woman who was covered in flour came to the ovens and rescued her bread.

"That smells divine," I said.

The cook—clearly the head cook—looked at me, perplexed.

"I come from cattle country," I said. "I have never smelled fresh bread in my life."

One moment, all the women in the room were wary—including Mena—and then next, as the cook's face transformed into a smile, everyone seemed to relax in the warm glow and scent of fresh bread.

"Honey!" the cook said imperiously. She set the bread down on the kitchen table and, using thick cloth mitts to hold it, took a bread knife and sliced into it. She slathered it with butter from a Thefarland village by the border, and then with honey. I watched both melt into the thick slice, and she handed it to me.

All of the women paused in cleaning up the porridge mess, or their other duties, and watched—holding their breath—as I took the slice in my burnt hands. I would not for the life of me show any signs that the heat of the bread hurt my fingers, not with what they'd just gone through, nor how tense the room had gotten. I took a bite of heaven. Whatever they saw on my face made the tension drop even further. And suddenly I found myself weeping at what these women must live with all the time.

These women would never say anything bad about their mistress—but it was clear that this one raging moment was not unusual. And they ended up comforting me.

"We've seen her rage like this before," the baker said, rather bravely. "We're used to it. It is far less now, and before, years before, it was less... rational. I'm sure it frightened you, being new to you."

"I've read about this sort of thing," I said. "Does she always get a headache after?"

"Yes, most times. Not always."

The baker patted my back and put more fresh bread on my plate. Another girl made me a Yezginy tea that was green, rich, and woke me up.

"The bread is better, but this is amazing!" I said.

"It's a gift from Lord Marce, but her ladyship doesn't care

for it. She often would get headaches afterward. She prefers herbal infusions."

I sipped the tea. I wondered if the stimulant qualities of the tea set off the headaches.

I knew that Ravantha's rage was not something they were truly used to, or they would not have scattered, hearing her storm down to their sanctum. Why should they be? I recalled that Palecu wrote that some people with head injuries were listless and did not thrive. Perhaps an impulsive temper was preferable. He'd written that the early stages were difficult, at times—which was one of the reasons Tages had supposed that where the brain was injured might be informative. There were some who had to re-learn how to function. Any sign of frustration might, in those cases, not only show symptoms of the damage, but a will to live and something to celebrate in early stages. It would take very secure people tending them to see that, and not forget the dangerous reality of aggravation outside the sick room. I was both saddened and cheered that these women were not used to their mistress's rages.

Mena was about to put the analgesic tea back into my bag when I spoke up. "This tea—it is good for her headaches. Leave it out. If you have balm, you can add it to her herbal teas as well."

The women nodded and were grateful. I left the room, much later, having discovered a refuge Ravantha rarely ventured into. I was careful with it, however, or she would have destroyed the comfort of all those who ventured to the kitchen.

Chapter Twelve

———⟪•⟫———

It was with extreme reluctance that Ravantha let me go back to Tages. I felt watched through part of my journey through her lands. After about three hours of my spine crawling, I stopped. I couldn't stand it.

I rarely intentionally touched any spirit world, except when I'd worked with Grandmother Turani, years ago, or sometimes when attempting techniques of divination Tages had shown me, yet without the results he seemed to require. This time, I thought of something I'd learned from Kutu, and his Hunter Cult—a cult that focused primarily on legends of animals, and how they moved and acted.

It came to mind, probably because of how both Crow and Jackal had been pacing me more frequently during my travels.

Kutu once told me stories where his whole body changed, and he seemed like the animals his fellow hunters had once hunted. He also told me that they believed in the Spirit of the animals, and I knew I wanted the help of a creature that was crafty and intelligent. I wondered if it would matter or even work—I *had* failed my adept test—but once I'd spent three hours on the road feeling like prey after enduring a sense of being caged in Ravantha's house, I couldn't help but reach out with a sense of power Grandmother Turani had taught me years ago.

I muttered some words in Ndeb, asking to join the byways of not just the jackal pack I'd heard nearby, but Jackal, the spirit of the jackals, himself. Even predators needed to hide from their prey, as well as those that preyed upon them. After a few deep breaths, Jackal came to my eyes. I knew him to be more than any jackal. I wondered at how quickly he'd answered my call, and wondered how often he lingered nearby.

I thought of the times I'd heard a lone jackal, laughing in the woods nearby.

He stepped forward, almost prancing his steps toward me, and then stopped, and seemed to do that bowing stretch, forelegs out, head down like any dog. There seemed, for a moment, to be something in this gesture, but I was too surprised to take time to understand it.

"Healer," he said, seeming to savor the title, "why do you call me?" he asked when he straightened. "You are not a hunter."

My heart pounded with my audacity. This was similar to meeting a god, which in some ways he was. I hadn't even been sure my request would work!

"I am being hunted," I said.

"You would not call the Deer, or Fowl?" he asked.

I waved the staff, which Ravantha had forced upon me. "I prefer a position of power."

"Indeed, Sen of the Woods," he said. I was shocked he knew my name. He laughed. "Like the hunter out in the woods, who must use the cunning of a jackal to outwit the more powerful? Or what you perceive, currently, as more powerful? Would that you look upon this moment one day, and laugh."

I did not understand what he meant by the last phrase. I said, "I had a friend who once told me a story about using trickery, yes."

He sniffed me. "A hunter who taught you to use acacia branches to guard yourself when you travel alone, perhaps?"

"Yes."

He smiled, a roguish smile, but one that was between a snarl and a grin. "He is one of the few who do not see us as cowards. That's for strangers, and those who would like to diminish our people, or what we represent. No *kaross* skins like rugs for his feet."

I shuddered at the thought of him being a rug, or any of his people.

"You are in need of cunning, I think, against forces using more power than you choose to take. Like your friend Kutu, who uses a jackal's cunning to evade the lion pride near his home—a pride that would attack him, his children, or his cattle."

"You are more clever than Lion," I said, feeding his pride.

"Indeed. But do you not walk often in the realm of nature?"

"I do. Often. Though," I said, looking about, "perhaps not quite like this." I realized I was in his world; within his perspective of the nature we were both part of. "Nature *is* how I do my healing art, the Medicine we do. It is by *your* gifts, and those of your fellows—plants and animals alike—that I learn from."

"You speak the Old Tongue well, like the gods and your sisters and aunts before you." He paused. "You are not like the healers... or hunters I have met on the Road, of late."

Somehow, I knew that the Road was not the path I was on, but the journey of nature, of the whole land moving and changing and growing. It was not even a good translation of what word he had used. It was only the best one I knew. It spoke to a movement, a Divine movement of greater magnitude than nature or gods, like a flow of a river.

"Am I not?" I asked, also wondering how and when to ask about my sisters.

His hackles rose, and his face took on a snarl. "No. You are something different, Sen of the Woods, not of this realm, nor truly the one you walk. I will lead you. But do not let your master know of this, for I would not act kindly to him. Or your hunter friend. They would have to pay a price for passage that you do not."

I let him lead me. I felt a fool. I wondered if, despite his words, I had paid a price for this passage, or would. I could not understand what Jackal meant. It was an interesting journey all the same, as we faded from my watcher's view. He showed me plants I had not yet put in my book. He gave me time to draw them and take notes.

"Do not gather these plants from here," he warned, "except in dire need, and only with their permission."

I looked at the plant and realized that it, too, had a Spirit guarding it. I nodded and drew.

Jackal sat beside me, watching me work with a sense of curiosity that did not get my hackles up the way Ravantha's keen observations did. His attention was no less intense, but it was fascination and a curiosity I could respect. He showed me more than plants but spoke a bit on the nature of This Way—though his words were in the words of a Jackal tongue that my spirit seemed to understand. If I were to describe it, the words would be as close to those describing any road I'd walked before.

I do not know how long the walk took. It felt as if it was hours, if not years, and no time at all. Jackal seemed to take on a role of showing me how his world—his kind and his prey's kind—was interwoven into the world of humans, and even that of ancestors. This weaving underlay not merely my healing art, but another side of a spirit-like world I had not seen in this way.

"You are as strong as the ancestors," I said, even though I'd never seen the world from their perspective, but I had seen their strong influence.

"You would do well in your form as a healer, Sen of the Woods, to see that."

He left me near Grandmother Turani's house. I had not thought to go there, but he bowed to my home as if to a temple it once had been. I briefly wondered at temples becoming houses of prostitution, or... homes.

I was far too shaken at my audacity, by this point, and what I had learned or gained. That thought faded with a great deal of trembling that led me to my old bed. I tried to put it down in my journal, but my hands shook.

All my attempts to write it down were futile. It was more than quivering hands. I had no words for it in Ndeb. I thought of the stories Kutu had shared with me. I thought of Jackal's Road, and how Grandmother Turani had taught me of the three colors of a Doctor-Diviner's healing Medicine. She had once said there were three Rivers, or even Roads, or Ways of meaning as well.

"I can only teach you one, preparing you for one of your teachers," she had said. "You may find, in the future, others who would teach you more." She had looked archly at me and laughed wickedly. "You will be surprised at your teachers, I think."

"Tages?" I asked her.

She had laughed hard at that one. "No. Though he will be your teacher, he's not surprising at all, though what you learn from him would certainly astonish all of his more foolish colleagues."

"Well-spoken Ndeb perplexes his colleagues?" I said.

She had laughed again.

It was her laughter that returned to me now as I trembled. I now wondered if one of those teachers might be Jackal. He had taught me a great deal, and he was—honestly—quite the surprise as well! Jackal's respectful bow to my old home did remind me that there was a sense of refuge inside that stone-against-boulder home. I bowed to where Jackal had left me, thanking him, and then went inside to sleep.

The next morning, I woke up and remembered something Ravantha had told me. I looked everywhere and did not find any baby clothes. I found old herbs that I cleaned out, and pots of paint that had once been used to refresh the paintings on the main chamber's walls, as well as old plates and bowls for eating that I dusted off and used to make breakfast to fuel my continued search. Everything was as I'd left it the last time I'd stayed in the place. After a bit more searching, the only unexpected thing I found was Grandmother Turani's treasure box. I remembered it as full of mementos and traded jewelry and coins. I opened it.

In it lay tarnished bits of an old necklace. A couple of amber gems hung from small chains, and the other silver-backed amber.

I held it in my hands, so that it had a bit of curve, as if it were around a neck. The barest bits of silver from the small amber glimmered in the light from the doorway as my hands trembled.

I swallowed, then took a deep breath against drowning in confusion.

Why would Grandmother Turani have part of Thielle's necklace?

I could hear Jackal's laugh, but also Grandmother Turani's, as all my thoughts of my childhood hit the walls of the stone home I was in. This part of the necklace had been better kept than the one I'd seen in my dream-vision, the one in Thefare's treasure room. The silver was cleaner, but years of neglect had given it a bit of a tarnished hue.

My hands began to shake uncontrollably. The past two days had been far too much. I did not feel as if I were in this world, but another. One hand holding the necklace, I steadied myself on the stone. Slowly, carefully, I went to the cooking spot and made tea. I spilled half the water, nearly putting out my small fire, but I had to warm myself and calm my body's sense of shock.

I put my half of the broken necklace in my bag to put it away to calm myself. I needed to take a deep breath and think of the woman who had found me. I wondered if she had other hiding places I'd somehow missed. I couldn't think of any. This place was spare, and neglect had made it rougher than the round hut I lived in now in Tages's compound. Nature was taking over. Still, it felt more like home than any place I'd lived since. I knew that I could return here. A refuge for my unknown future.

What I could not return to was a sense that I understood or knew the woman who had raised me. My thoughts could find no purchase in what I'd known—each time I tried, I felt blank, so much so that I realized time had passed in the pause of my struggled thinking.

I shook my head and remembered I had made Tages a

promise. It was a relief to have something to do, even if it took me closer to the Westvell.

It was not that I couldn't find peace here—I left the place reluctantly—but I could not be at peace in my own mind. I turned to the one refuge I'd had for the past year: study. Jackal and the potential implications in a part of a necklace were too much. I retreated into the type of information that was equally intense and heady, but far more familiar.

I had to face that I might never become an adept. I could study and learn. I could also, apparently, walk in Jackal's Way. I'd still be able to help heal people, however I could.

I went back to the ruins of Jammon's city. It was a poor retreat, as much of the time it rained, and I could not work in my journal terribly well. I spent two nights there to take samples of the leaves and flowers and carefully pressed them in my press till I ran out of paper and blocks. I hoped my samples pressed and preserved well. I worked a bit frantically in the brief moments when rain did not fall. I had found one small place safe from the rain, and put my journal and press there just a little bit away from the place of the three chimneys. I found no other dry spot large enough for me. I slept a great deal more wet than I preferred.

I was thrilled when I woke up and the sky was blue. I drew the Tree now fully in bloom, but I was distressed to see more signs of disease on one side. I could see the top of the roots on that side were black with nothing good.

I sang as I drew, and the first eight lines of it came.
"One was wrapped
In lace and gold
Another leaves and dirt
One died in the cold

Apprentice

The other death did skirt

One was lost, another lives
Oh, the humble child
Into my arms did come..."

I felt the love of Grandmother Turani's arms. While some of the words came—gift and wild, and something that reminded me of the sound of a drum, roots, and death and breath came vaguely to my ears—the song remained incomplete.

The memory of that warm embrace, like sunlight sparkling beneath the canopy of a tree, smelling almost green and lush as the ground below, the ceremony of the Milk Tree came to my mind. Abandoned girl that I was—one severed from her mother by a choice to let me die. Here was this Tree at the site that reminded me of a half-remembered lullaby, and a feeling that made me believe that it was probably where I'd been left to perish.

And yet I had lived. This was no Milk Tree. It was a fruit tree, admittedly of a blossom I had only seen here. I could gather up symbolism similar to the ceremony of a Milk Tree, perhaps. I had been severed from my mother at this Tree.

I was my own woman.

Whatever label given to me now, or in the future: apprentice, adept, Doctor-Diviner, daughter, niece... it didn't matter. Those were nearly symbolic roles, like those given to dying gods—labels with loose truth and only for those I mattered to, not the person (or goddess) it adorned.

I knew that many girls were given their own tree before they went through their Milk Tree ceremony. That fruit-bearing tree was called a Milk Tree, because when it was cut, it bled white. The sap was known for making wine. A good one—and something now quite rare in an area known for liquor and other spirits, and a coastal region to both the west and east that was rich with wine from grapes. Overharvesting of the sap had killed many Milk Trees, and a blight had taken others. More proof of a dying and changing age? Losing the symbol to use in celebrations was sufficient reason for the ceremony to go out of regular practice.

I could be spiteful and say men overharvested that sap for their own ceremonies once a year, when they initiated young boys into manhood. It was also true that women let men overharvest the sap even from their own trees to earn money from the sale of that special wine. Add to that, there were other reasons for fewer ceremonies, other than any shift in ritual methodology. Symbols of self, power, and independence weren't romantic ideals currently carried into marriage.

I wondered if Hastia saw the ceremony this way, or if it was just another ceremony to get dressed up for. Unlike the past, where men moved to their wives' homes, now young women traveled to their husbands' villages and towns, leaving their maiden tree behind, if they even had one. She would normally have to leave her tree behind, except it was in some oversized pot.

From a song, which gave me a sense of loving embrace, I was now nettled.

I shook off my crabby mood and focused on my work. I looked up from my damp seat to the glorious blue sky, thankful for the first truly clear, rainless day in weeks. I gathered up leaves and fallen bark for my mentor to see. I then sat where I could draw some detailed studies in my journal. I spent a good three hours trying to capture various parts of the tree in my drawing, as well as the entire scene, like all my plant studies, but with added detail for identification. Without rain or even a promise of rain, I could indulge in detail.

I heard a sound and turned in a swirl of energy that Larce would have approved of—had I been armed. Tages stood there.

"I wanted to come see it for myself and thought you might be here," he said.

"How did you know?" I asked him.

"Being a Doctor-Diviner does include divining things, my dear," he said automatically. He paused, sighed. "I took a chance." There was a twinge of grief staining his face as he said it. "What were you humming?"

"Oh... I hadn't realized I was."

"And singing. Something about a humble child."

"It was a lullaby Grandmother Turani used to sing to me. How she saved me. I don't remember all the words. Maybe if I keep humming it, it will come back to me."

We sat back down, and he looked at my drawing. He studied it a long while, and there was an expression on his face I could not interpret, not even when I saw tears in the corner of his eyes.

"I think I erred during your adept test," he said.

"How?" I asked, wondering if I ought to be angry.

"Sen, do you know that I cannot see this Tree?"

Surprised by his words, I handed him the samples of bark, leaf, the last of the blossoms, and the beginnings of budding fruit. "Can you see these?"

"These, yes. Interesting."

I thought back to Jackal, and how he was mostly unseen by even hunters who might revere him. I thought about his admonishment that I not harvest while in his Way. Was this tree there? But I could see it here! Was this Tree, of all trees, like

Jackal was to all jackals? It was too young to my mind. How long
would it be before the rot on the other side of it overtook the tree?
Again, where was this Tree? That is... in which Way, or as
Grandmother Turani had put it, which River? She had said I must
learn and bind the three. I had not thought of it for so long, and it
hadn't made much sense at the time. I tried to recall what she had
said, however confusing it might have been!

One, I now realized, must be the White River, which I was
learning now; the Red that must be Jackal's Way; and the Black I
had not yet walked upon.

Or it might not be. Grandmother Turani's words were
more than enigmatic, but often unrelated from one train of
thought to another.

I had so much to learn! Yet here was my mentor who could
see the blossoms I had shown him, but not the Tree itself.

"How is it that I see this Tree when you cannot?" I asked.

"I do not know," Tages admitted. "If I'm honest, I am not
sure I ever would have, or could have."

This was disconcerting. I shifted the topic to something
else I found uncomfortable. "Who was Grandmother Turani?" I
asked him. "I found something in her home I cannot account for."

"What is it?"

"Something that reminds me of a myth, as if it comes from
one of the stories of the gods in this region. Part of an amulet," I
said, unwilling to consider calling this part of the broken necklace
anything else. I knew I was saying it terribly, but giving any hint to
some of the ideas I had was far too strange.

"When I came here as a young man—boy, actually—she
was already old. There were tales I heard of her having been there
for many ages. I once asked her about it, and she just laughed and

said, 'Those are just stories!'"

I smiled. "She often did not like stories about the dealings of gods, or she laughed at them."

He grinned and said, "No, she did not. She said that people rarely understand the whole of a god, that elements of a god's character got lost in a story, because people focused only on one tale, and too many had been lost or changed, so there was no hope of seeing the truth—except in real faith. She told me, 'In this age, myths and gods are dying things. We need a new way of knowing them.' This was before she'd found you, I think. I don't know if she'd said anything to you like this."

I shook my head but smiled.

Tages continued. "She did tell me something of importance, once: 'Faith isn't about the worship of a god's power, but exercising our power to participate in the tending of the people and the world around us, all given to us by the God of gods.'"

"Like helping the poor below Thefare's castle?"

"Yes. We would have done the work, regardless of any trade Thefare's factors could have offered us—if we are faithful to the way of the gods." He rubbed his white scar that showed he was a master of his art. "Perhaps I am lucky. It is not an attitude I've seen in many of our contemporary colleagues, but I have seen hints of it in some of the older books I've found—handwritten ones."

"The ones in Ndeb."

"The ones you've read, yes. What do you remember in them?" he asked me.

"That our role as Doctor-Diviners is as a symbol." I paused, thinking of the broken part of the necklace I had in my bag, and how I saw others view the other part. "It's either something to claim and make use of..." I paused. "I know I could quote you the words. I think I remember them, but I wish to relate it to what I'm seeing now."

"Go on," he said.

"Some symbols are used as a standard, like a crown or a flag, something to hold up for one's own purpose—but that might defy what the symbolic meaning actually is."

I thought about the living and dying Tree in front of us. Stories I knew would never offer any singular meaning.

"Such as?" he asked, and I could see that he was still testing my knowledge.

"Bathos. I'm glad to have met him only once. He uses his Doctor-Diviner scars as symbols to let him practice. It's a sign of power, but he brings nothing to it and does not give respect to the symbol itself. He does not work to support it, nor does he support the people whom he makes ill in his shoddy practice. He hides behind the symbol of his scars."

"Interesting. What of Cai? You must know he does not have your curiosity. Skill, yes, more than plenty for me to be proud to have had some of his education. Aule does. My own son has more than enough intelligence. He will not have the white scar of a Master Doctor-Diviner."

"But *they* do the work. Cai will always respect the patient he tends, as will Aule."

"And then this amulet—yes, I can still see some things, but I confess not clearly. I can almost feel the shape of the thing, but..." He shrugged. "You say you found it in Turani's home? Does that change what you know of her?"

I thought for a moment. "No, I guess not. I am thinking

that I do not understand the symbol, but I am reminded of the *value* of a symbol—and that it can be misused."

"Perhaps a good thing to know, in this time." He looked up at a Tree he could not see. "Tell me about Ravantha," he said.

I did not see this as a random request. I was, for one, highly symbolic to her.

"She is still in pain from her rape. She does not trust men often."

"Can she be healed?"

"I do not know. I know that the injury she had surely injured her brain. I've seen more evidence of irrational behavior—not a great deal, mind you, but enough. Fuluns obviously hit her head against the stones of the treasure room repeatedly, and hard enough to silence her into unconsciousness."

"How do you know he hit her like that?" he asked. "Did she tell you?"

"No, I..." How could I tell him I'd seen it in a vision, *without* the ceremonial practice of divination? I had not passed his initiatory test. I gave a helpless shrug and tried to speak the words, but they remained too intimately invasive to Ravantha, and I'd betrayed her in my thoughts far too much already. No one needed the details.

"She was, you know, hit like that," he said. "I helped heal her from her injuries. Her father took her from here as soon as possible—despite my belief she ought not be moved, and such haste surely caused yet more damage as they traveled. Either a cart or horse would not help."

"You knew that before you read Vesalus," I said. "Even though her scalp wasn't bleeding?"

"Oh, the skin was broken, but her skull felt intact. If there was a crack, it was not something that allowed for any release of pressure."

"So, the cart or horse her father took her home with would have added to that internal damage," I said.

He nodded. "As we see now. I could not trepan her then—her father did not see any wound on her head, which had cleaned up quickly. The wounds seemed minor to his eyes, and his experience in some fighting did not allow for any other possibility. He did not accept that there could be trauma *inside* the skull that could cause damage. Eighteen years ago, the thought that there could be that kind of injury was not contemplated by many."

"It's not now. It would have been better if it had bled, reducing the pressure."

"Trepanning would have been the only option. I could have done it without causing infection."

"He rejected your help. Though you were already a renowned Doctor-Diviner?"

"He had seen too many injuries in his time of war, when he was a young man, being a younger son. Most of his battles were on the great island of Dedathon across the waters to the east. Of course, he doubted me. I hadn't witnessed any battle injuries, living peacefully in Obrone."

I shook my head. "Palecu and Vesalus proved you right."

"Far too late, even if a man like Rasce would even *read* books like that."

"Regardless, there's little we can do to repair the damage now. But there's more. I'm not sure that *my* presence will help her. I'm more like a thorn stuck in the wound."

"I wondered. I was hoping seeing you on a daily basis would get that part of her troubles out of her system."

"It didn't!" I said, gesturing my frustration.

"You're bruised!" he said, when movement revealed my arm.

"She has Larce and Marce training me with a staff."

"Not a bad idea."

"Oh?"

I was about to ask about Marce's hand tremors, but Tages smiled and teased. "There are often animals in the wild who might like to make a meal of you," he said.

"And I've been wandering around the woods so long without being able to defend myself?" I asked, not hiding the sarcasm in my tone.

"I've neglected you a bit, my dear. Cai was often around. And two are better than one."

"Can I ask if you communicated with Aranthur?"

"Yes. He wrote me—as I gather he does with many others of various abilities—but I realized that I could not help him."

"Why not?"

"Because I had divined, years before, and discovered the thread of it through his ancestors, that it is an inherited disorder. One cannot appeal to them to remove it, and all other minor doctors would be equally doomed as they remain unhealed themselves."

"Are the symptoms hand tremors and an unsteady gait?"

"Quite right, Sen. How do you know?"

"Observation. I believe Marce must have it."

Tages nodded. "Only the gods might aid him now."

I thought of the necklace and wondered if that was what all the fuss was about. Reaching for it had caused so much trouble, and what could a broken bauble do? Most likely, he believed it would heal him or heal his son and reverse the doom of his lineage.

"You have made some noteworthy observations, Sen. I have lately thought to have you visit various villages on your own to do healing work."

"Oh?" I was not yet an adept.

"You are good enough."

"Thank you. When? And which ones?"

We discussed which towns might need a mere student's attention. I noticed he had me traveling to the Westvell as well as some of the towns north. "Westvell again?"

"I know you'd be safe there, traveling alone."

"Ravantha does not like me being an independent woman."

He laughed. "You are not. You are an apprentice bound to me."

"But this feels more like adept work," I said.

"Yes, I know." He looked me in the eye and said, "Will you accept that I have in the past reasons to not have given you your adept scar, even while you are doing the work?"

"I think so," I said. I wanted to continue working and studying with Tages, but I had to admit, the idea of not getting the elevation while doing actual adept work made me chafe a little. Yet I was glad I was working on my own comparative taxonomy project. There might be more then, than not having passed his initiatory requirements. Apparently, I'd not stop learning. Was I... Could I be content with that?

"Truly, Sen, I had my reasons. The less perceived autonomy you had, the more authority I have over you in the eyes of others. I could not divine the right path, especially after your initiatory test. But I think you must have some of your own now.

Tell me what you know of Thielle, as we just spoke of symbols, and gods as symbols as well. What does she symbolize to you?"

"She is of beauty and love."

"Yes, and for a Doctor-Diviner, what is she?"

"Spring, herbs..." I realized he was looking for something a little less common. "Harmony."

"Yes. What do we bring with our healing, with our Medicine?"

"Harmony to the body. Harmony to the community. Ah!" I said with some understanding of his aim. Beauty and love were popular, and overt signs of a deeper significance that I had passed over.

"You, for some reason, hold an almost symbolic importance to two people, and I have considered, and yes, I use that word with purpose, that it could disrupt not merely my own household, but that discord could extend to the larger community harmony. As Thielle and many gods, including her sister, Nhor, are of healing and harmony, I must do what I can to promote it. If I gave you more autonomy, they would potentially make use of this freedom, and that would add to disharmony."

With his words, I could see flashes in the darkness of fighting, and heard wails of pain and frustration, and tasted the salt of many tears.

"I do see that," I said reluctantly, damping down my disappointment.

"However, I need you as an adept. I am getting older, and Velia deserves my attention."

I snorted. "Master, you merely want to stay in your room and study with the tools Aule gave you. I know that machine he brought Velia distracted her from the wealth of information."

Looking at him, I could see the age I had not noticed before. He moved as if his joints pained him. His beard was now more salt than pepper. The worry lines between his brows were now as deep as those around his eyes. He was not as spry as he once was. The lines in his face now spoke volumes, and as if in clear writing, I could read his fear.

"Sen, long before Cai came to me, my vision began to fade, like the old men unable to hunt because they cannot see as far. Velia knows some of this, but I cannot bear to tell her this. I am losing my power."

I thought, *You have not lost your skill, Tages. You have not lost your considerable knowledge.* I couldn't speak the words. I was breathless with shock.

He said, "The more I can study the materials Aule brings me, including the books, the more I can teach you!" He prodded my head. "You are among the best students I have had. You like the past and the present forms of healing, fascinated by both. Your choice to do the study you have chosen is a very, very good one. It is inspired. The time you spent in the Westvell helped me see that knowledge can be a way forward, such as you use it, and I am learning to use it."

He took a deep breath, staring at the place where I'd told him the Tree stood. His fingers moved over the texture of the bark, and then he looked at the piece with yet more study.

Finally, he spoke again. "More, I think we must consider *how* you might do divination. It is also clear to me that you see far more of the unseen than I ever could, and without needing that mushroom. Your time as an adept will be a time for me to learn new ways. Together, we can strive to keep harmony in our community, and healing."

During the conversation, I felt incredibly young, naive, and inexperienced. What I'd done with Ravantha was still a wound, purging my pride like pus. I wanted to be humble and accept anything Tages said. Toward the end, I laughed. I felt as if I could return to familiar and safer ground.

"I look forward to it. Has Aule written about the extracts we made? Have they done any more studies at the university?"

"Yes, and I will see what I can learn. Go gather some plants, and when you come home, I will share his letters with you. Professor Cuintus sent you another book. If he weren't married, I would think he was courting you. Are you sure you would not wish to live with his family and continue your studies with him? I must confess I can only guide you so much as I have done. No more. I am human, apparently, first before I am a Doctor-Diviner."

"As much as I value his books, his art has little to do with the spirit side of ours. I do believe you continue to have that in you. For my own study, I have more plants and drawings added to my comparative study," I said.

"I am very proud of what you have done so far. Science and lore joined together!"

"Then, I have your blessing to continue? To make something of it?"

"Of course!" he said. "It will be part of your unique Mastery as a Doctor-Diviner."

"Speaking of lore, could an ancestor be fueling Ravantha's pain?" I asked.

"Possibly, but is she neglecting them? You lived with her for weeks."

"Not that I could see, though she focuses on the women of her family's line, such as her grandmother, who lived in her manor before her. I did not notice any spirits, if that's what you mean. Perhaps you divined the problem?"

"I have tried. Observation served. I could not see anything of that—her pain is something she clings to, and who is to blame her for that? I did think it was being fed—that her pain was being fed."

"I can see that," I said, "having watched her. But by whom I do not know, except herself. I must say that she eats greedily at that plate, whoever hands it to her." I tried to hope it wasn't Marce or Larce. They seemed to have some loyalty toward her.

He nodded. "I agree. What healing Medicine we could create for her, from ritual to herbs, it would never work if she feeds off what poisons her wounds, it poisons her mind. She must give it up to heal."

I contemplated him for a while. "I think there are times I will never understand divination as well as you do."

"It is a difficult art, for many reasons. You cannot be guided by what you want to know. You must balance what you perceive with knowledge to interpret. I do not think it is something you need to worry about mastering as long as you continue your studies. You do well enough as it is. I have never found fault with your practice." He paused. "You see more than I knew. This Tree you see confirms more than the mushroom did— or rather, I did not understand what you said when everything remained the same, but louder. Because I am seeing a flower in my hands from a tree that I cannot perceive, says all I need to know. You are more than ready."

Under a Tree that Tages could not see, he gave me my adept scar. We both had a supply of white clay, but he gave me his so that it would heal clean and white on my bronze skin. My first task as an adept was to ensure this would heal properly.

He left soon after, wanting to get back to his own work. I would be his eyes and ears on the land, while he stayed in his laboratory.

I sat under the Tree, with blossoms in my hair, listening to ants eat bark on its rotting far side. I knew that being found here was perhaps not a Milk Tree ceremony, but it had changed me. I looked at my adept scar, brushed a flower petal over it. I thought, *Now I can travel even further, gain more knowledge of the world, and rise to Mastery.*

There was a flutter of wings. I looked up. Crow was there, playing with her amber-beaded bauble, glinting like gold in the sunlight. She grasped it with her claws and laughed at me. Jackal, somewhere to the north, echoed her laugh.

"What does that even mean?" I asked. "Why do you laugh?"

"You'll see," said Crow.

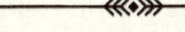

E • N • D

About the Author

Mab Morris lives in Dahlonega, Georgia, with a number of cats and a Celtic labyrinth of her own design. Her storytelling and her love of fantasy began at a very young age, where she was drawn to Ursula K. Le Guin and J.R.R. Tolkien. Mythology, history, and folklore are her passion.

She writes mystical fantasy books set in the past, present and future of the world of Ihyel, where demi-gods and mortals alike struggle with their fate. She also writes the murder-mysteries of The Bone Reader, about Cemirowl who speaks with the dead, and the Regency adventures of gender-fluid spy Alex Goodward.

Check out www.mabmorris.com for more info.

Other Books by Mab Morris

――――――――――― ≪•≫ ―――――――――――

Lost Bones

Book One of The Bone Reader

Cemirowl is gifted, and cursed. She sees the spirits of the dead, and sees the future in her basket of bones; her sight is cryptic, lacking, and mostly useless. In her tiny village, she is a priestess, but still an object of curiosity and an outcast.

A chance meeting brings one of the king's caballiers to her door for a reading, for nothing more than some entertainment. He is well-entertained indeed by her predictions of his lady loves... and far less so when she foretells a coming death. He leaves, dismissing her. But for all that her power is mysterious and often confusing, it is never, ever wrong.

When Queen Tidyri is murdered, the caballiers return for Cemirowl. She is brought unwillingly into the palace and into a web of intrigue and lies, where King Larthor rages in his grief. He demands that Cemirowl now use her gifts to find the one who killed his beloved wife.

Cemirowl must draw on all her abilities – her powers, no matter how unreliable; her intuition for reading people; her knowledge; and her wits – to discover the murderer, lay the spirits of the dead to rest, and help the living to grieve and find peace. And, perhaps, she will finally find a place where she belongs.

LOST BONES is a fantastical murder mystery set in the rich world of Ihyel, where the hard-won peace between two kingdoms rests on the shoulders of one determined, compassionate priestess.

Fate of the Red Queen

A Standalone Novel in the World of Ihyel

"I am not defeated! If my body falls, it is only that alone which dies!"

Faced with a war she could not win, the Red Queen sealed her country's fate with her final sacrificial pledge. Yezgyin was locked into undeath, the people and their enemies alike cursed to neither live nor die unless the spell could one day be broken.

Centuries passed, and history faded into legend. Kuen, a newly anointed Red Nun, escapes a vicious attack on her convent, and flees into the Jungle of the Dead. Amid the ruins of lost Yezgyin, she mourns the death of her mentor and all she has known, utterly lost to her grief. But the jungle whispers of her, and its otherworldly inhabitants welcome her as their new Red Queen, the one who will break their curse.

Kuen must find her way through the demands of the past and the hopes of the future, as the Red Queen's ancient adversary returns to win the war that never ended. With the life and death of Yezgyin at stake, she must fight for her own fate, or she and the people of the Jungle will never truly live again.

FATE OF THE RED QUEEN is a standalone novel set in the mysterious world of Ihyel.